CHARADE

★

JOHN MORTIMER

VIKING

VIKING
Penguin Books Ltd, Harmondsworth, Middlesex, England
Viking Penguin Inc., 40 West 23rd Street, New York, New York 10010, U.S.A.
Penguin Books Australia Ltd, Ringwood, Victoria, Australia
Penguin Books Canada Limited, 2801 John Street, Markham, Ontario, Canada L3R 1B4
Penguin Books (N.Z.) Ltd, 182–190 Wairau Road, Auckland 10, New Zealand

First published by The Bodley Head 1947
Published by Viking 1986

Copyright © Advanpress Ltd, 1947, 1986

Reproduced, printed and bound in Great Britain by
Hazell Watson & Viney Limited,
Member of the BPCC Group,
Aylesbury, Bucks
Typeset in Monotype Bembo

British Library Cataloguing in Publication Data

Mortimer, John, 1923–
Charade.
I. Title
823'.914[F]   PR6025.07552
ISBN 0-670-81186-6

CONTENTS

to

CLIFFORD *and* KATHLEEN MORTIMER

This story is designed to serve a purpose entirely of its own and the descriptions in it have no direct reference to the organization of the armed forces or film industries of this or any other country

I

Arrival

THIS WAS where I used to come, as a child, for holidays. As I looked out of the train window I recognized paths and tunnels among the cliffs. On some of the sheer faces soldiers were stretched out like specimen butterflies. The town was, as I always remembered it, shrouded in rain.

The train turned a corner and I saw that they had broken the pier in half. Had I been promising myself a go on the 'dodgems'? Certainly I felt disappointed.

The rain had greased the promenade. It veiled the bandstand and fell in a mist round the barbed wire. I wondered if there were still song birds in the breakfast room of the Princess Royal.

For the last time I stood up in the carriage and looked at myself in the glass over the photograph of 'High Street, God-alming'. My father would have approved of my clothes. The hard white collar, school tie and blue suit were essential at an insurance office. But were they right for my new job? I had bought a cloth cap and, if I found that it was customary, I meant to put it on back to front.

I took a magazine entitled *Kinema Arts, A Bilingual Quarterly*, from my attaché case and carried it ostentatiously in my hand. I expected to be met on the platform.

In this expectation I was deceived. I spent the next half-hour trying to find a taxi. During this time I accosted a hearse, two doctors and a young officer who was sitting in the front of a square Daimler with a lady. As I put my head in the window

and asked if he was engaged he motioned me violently away
and appeared to draw his service revolver. His was a face I
was to recognize later.

I set off to walk to the hotel, the rain soaking my trousers
and raising blisters on the shiny cover of *Kinema Arts*. Hadn't
the Action Film Unit been telegraphed?

I saw the familiar hotel through a gauze curtain of rain.
Splashing up the marble steps I could hear the twitter of birds
from the breakfast-room and felt reassured. I was even more
reassured by the sight of the hall porter, whom I recognized
from my boyhood, sitting in his box reading one of the
Waverley Novels. I went up to the desk and gave my name.
The receptionist disappeared into some recess and I gazed back
at the lounge, waiting for his return.

How well I remembered it! The elderly waiters trundled the
tea about with the solemn unconcern of nurses wheeling
patients to the operating theatre. The lady asleep, whose green
eye-shield almost touched the bosom of her dress, I was almost
sure I recognized. Under the ferns stood the writing table at
which I had sat as a child reading, when it was too early to go
out to the cinema, the same copy of *Crockford's Clerical
Directory* the little girl was now using for code cricket. Some
of the guests I had even met before. An actress, a friend of my
mother's, who stayed here every year, was having tea with
her two brothers. She was an extremely dignified old lady
dressed in powder blue, who had excited me once by her
very respectable reminiscences of the theatre. Both her brothers
were in the Church.

It was all just as it had always been, except, in one corner,
there were signs that they had had to have the workmen in.
A group of men in overalls and felt hats were sitting round
with bags of tools. The only thing that seemed strange for
this hotel was that the workmen were being served with the
usual plates of infinitesimal sandwiches.

The receptionist returned, switched on his green-shaded lamp and looked at me through his pince-nez.

'Who booked this room for you?'

This was the moment to bring out proudly the name of the Action Film Unit; but so confused was I by the sudden familiarity of the place that I murmured, as I would have done on arriving here from school twelve years ago:

'My mother.'

'Oh, that's all right. We were afraid you had some connection with the film people. Between you and me we aren't thinking of letting any more of those ladies and gentlemen in.'

He gave a titter which I found sadistic and then called the hall porter to take me up to my room.

The lift still seemed to work by hand. The porter, who was hunch-backed, pulled on a rope running through the cage, and we mounted stealthily through the shaft. Whether he was aided by any sort of mechanism I don't know; but certainly he had to make great efforts. Pulling on the rope he looked like a sexton gleefully tolling a knell. Peering round at me he asked if I was anything to do with the pictures.

'Not yet,' was all I thought it safe to say before I got the general climate of opinion.

'Director's wife reckons I ought to be on the pictures. Some picture about Notre Dame she reckons I ought to be on.' And then, as I didn't reply: 'They don't want for nothing, them on the pictures. Don't want for nothing she was telling me.'

As I got out he clanged the gates behind me, laughed theatrically and sank from view. I made a mental note that the director's wife must be a woman of little tact.

In my room I took off my starched shirt and changed it for a soft one of dark blue which my Uncle James had bought for a Mediterranean cruise—my mother had found it about after his death. Then I went downstairs again, halving my time by walking. There was still no sign of the Film Unit, and I sat down to wait. The tea had disappeared and most of the guests were now asleep. Only the workmen had produced dice, and my mother's old friend was sitting up before her glass-topped table, her hair piled majestically on her head, playing that elaborate patience which she had taught me all one wet afternoon when I was eleven, and which I never remembered. She recognized me at once, and I sat down opposite her, glad of someone to whom I could talk and confess my nervousness about my new job.

'Down here for your holiday? Drat. I need a red ten . . .'

'Well, no. As a matter of fact I've got a job.'

'Insurance?'

'No. That was what my father wanted, you know. But I've always been interested in the cinema, the serious cinema, of course, and mother had an old friend in the Action Film Unit . . .'

'My dear boy. How exciting.'

'Yes, it is, rather.'

'I'll always remember when I felt the call. Black queen. The bishop said that when he cast me as the forequarters of the ass in our little Nativity play he never knew what seeds he was sowing. Do you think this is cheating? But as Dame Ethel said before she died, My dear, she said, your life in the theatre might have been one long Nativity play. So sweet of her, I thought. Can I move these up if I promise to move them down again the moment I get a black nine? What part have you got? Walking on?'

'Oh no. I'm not acting. They say in their letter that I shall start as the director's assistant.'

'I don't remember we had that post in the theatre. The director of the Schiller Theatre in Godesburg had several assistants I believe; but they were young ladies, and none of them

quite the thing, you know. I think I'm making it come out.
I do hope I shan't feel guilty about it.'

'I don't really know what I am expected to do at first. But
anyway, I shall be learning the whole time.'

'I can't tell you. I know so little about films. Of course,
I've never been. Sarah, I believe, once had herself photo-
graphed as Josephine. She said she found the cinema people
most peculiar. And anyone *she* found peculiar . . . !'

'Don't you think things may have changed?'

'Oh, everything changes. Young ladies now, I believe, wear
their make-up *off* the stage.'

'Yes, but these aren't ordinary entertainment films. The
Action Film Unit photographs real subjects, taken from life.
Down here they are making a story about the army training
on the beaches. Later on we shall be photographing the troops
in action. It's not just the usual escapist American stuff.'

'You mean—sort of plays with a purpose?'

'Well . . .'

'A dear bishop sometimes wrote those for us. We'd perform
them for charity on Sunday afternoons. I never remember
them as being very profitable.'

'Films that make people think,' I said rather smugly, 'are
never as profitable as . . .'

'It *is* coming out. Do you know, it's almost an anticlimax.'
Nevertheless she went on piling the cards on to the aces and
then looked at me, smiling. 'You're just as serious as your
mother,' she went on. 'She really believed in her sculpture,
and yet she gave it up to marry your father. Now, I believe,
she does none at all. I used to see a lot of her at one time, when
she was at the Art School and I was playing in the Repertory
Theatre. Those were the days when I first met Mr. Henry
Cooper.' (She always referred to her husband, an actor who
first lost his memory and then died, in this rather formal
manner.) 'Yes, I had just met Mr. Henry Cooper and your

mother was very friendly with a young painter—there's a
man staying at the hotel now who puts me very much in
mind of him, although a great deal older, of course—and we
used to go to plays together. Your mother dearly loved the
theatre and now, I suppose, she wants to get in touch with it
again through you.'

'But it isn't the theatre.'

'I know, dear, but I can't help hoping that one day some
London manager, Forbes perhaps, or Mathieson, I never know
who's still about, will see one of your films and give you a
job. Nice as it may be I can't feel the cinema is really the
legitimate.'

As her brothers had gone to bed early I took Mrs. Cooper
in to dinner. I think she might have warned me about the hotel
food, or I might have guessed something for myself by the
enormous number of pots, tins and paper-bags she kept at her
table. In my childhood I remembered staggering across this
dining-room surfeited. Now I was hardly presented with the
rudiments of a snack. The regular visitors were obviously
prepared for this and for the most part they ate their own
provender without complaint. Mrs. Cooper made a hearty
meal off biscuits and meat paste and little rounds of breakfast
sausage; but did not find it necessary to offer anything to me.
I remember watching, with envy, a major at the next table
who was dining with a lady. He had come in carrying some
cold game-bird by the legs; and he and his friend were now
sharing it ravenously. He was rather a bulky, fresh-com-
plexioned man of about fifty, whom I was to get to know a
great deal better. He always looked cheerful, except on one
fateful occasion which I shall describe later, and he looked
particularly cheerful that evening. The woman he was with
was small and pretty and seemed in great awe of the waiters.

During the long intervals between the token courses I had
time to look round for the Film Unit. I saw the workmen,

still wearing their hats, at a distant table, apparently still dicing and drinking bottled beer. But there was no one whom I could possibly connect with my new job. I asked Mrs. Cooper if she had seen any film people about the hotel. 'There are some rather strange newcomers,' she said. 'At first I took them for holiday-makers. They always seem to affect sun-bathing costume, with tinted spectacles and so on; although, goodness knows, the weather hasn't given them any encouragement. My brothers said they might be the film people, but they move about so quickly that no one can be sure.'

And that was all I learnt from her that evening.

After dinner she went upstairs with one of those large volumes of theatrical reminiscences she got from Boots' library. Before she went she said:

'The entertainment world is all a sort of dream. You only wake up when you fail, or when you succeed.'

'But this isn't entertainment. It's real,' I tried to tell her; but she had already made her exit, her chin high, her fingers just holding the knee of her dress, up the long dark staircase to bed.

I went out to the cinema. The film was old and extremely bad. At first I felt an enjoyable superiority in criticizing it from the standpoint of the Action Film Unit whose films were coherent, socially valid and sincere. But half-way through its very badness got a grip on me. I was forced into an interest in the shoddy, unlikely story and compelled, in spite of myself, to keep my eyes on the screen. I could feel the excitement spreading in the shadows around me, where the lovers were sprawled together, clutching hands and knees and eating sweets. Part of the fascination of the film, for me at any rate, lay in a girl who was playing quite a minor part. Her voice—it was an English film—had the pathetic snootiness of a well-brought-up child. Her smile was childishly both guilty and defiant. It was as if she had done something rather shameful and would never be able to play with really nice children again. She wore simple clothes, and the hair fell straight down one side of her face. I found the sight of her so exciting that for the last quarter of an hour I was praying that the film would never stop nor her reflection ever disappear from the screen. I often have this experience in cinemas: I forget everything, my critical sense leaves me, my eyes fill with tears and I am convinced by the cheapest pathos and consumed by the crudest desires. I remember this film particularly as it was the first that I saw as a member, however remote, of the industry, and in more ways than one it seemed to cloud my judgment and upset my emotions, leaving me in a half-drugged condition from which, during my time with the Film Unit, I never really recovered.

However, as I say, I was sorry when the film ended. The appearance of a short documentary, made to encourage owners of electric grills not to throw away their old toasting-forks, but put them neatly out for salvage, failed to soothe me. I walked out into the rain and blackout, over-excited and extremely hungry. I got back to my room and undressed before the long wardrobe mirror. As I lay beneath the pink satin quilt and read *Kinema Arts* my feeling of excitement died away. So did the warmth. Only hunger remained. I decided to ring the bell for the chambermaid and make an appeal for sandwiches.

For a long time there was no answer. Then I heard footsteps in the passage and the sound of singing. My door opened and I saw a girl in a black dress standing just outside the range of my bedside light.

'Oh, good evening,' I said. 'Have you, by any chance, anything to eat?'

'Yes,' she said. She shot her arm into the light and I saw her vermilion nails clasped round a greasy bag. 'Have a chip.'

Although this wasn't the sort of service the hotel had once given, I appreciated her personal kindness.

'I bet you're hungry. Doesn't the food here stink?'

'Well, I wouldn't say that.'

'I would.'

'I should have thought, if you were working . . .'

'That's what I say. But *they* don't. They feed us the same as those old corpses in the lounge. We go out to the pub every evening. Then we have chips on the way home.'

She advanced into the light and stood uncertainly. Then she sat heavily down on the bed beside me. She was certainly pretty, her high forehead and small, contemptuous nose reminded me of the girl in the film; only this one seemed older, she had been kept for longer away from the nice children. As she sat down I was too surprised to notice she wore a diamond ring, or that her plain, black dress fitted her extremely well.

'Trouble is, I get tight every night.'

'And they don't mind?'

'Who doesn't mind?'

'The hotel?'

'Now why on earth should they? Only thing is . . . I can never remember which is my husband's bedroom.'

I didn't want her to go on in this strain. We had eaten the last chip and I asked, rather sharply:

'Can't you get me something else to eat? Out of the hotel, I mean.'

'You *are* greedy, aren't you? No. I shouldn't say I could. I shouldn't say the hotel people like me very much.'

'Perhaps not if you get drunk every night. But I am sure you could get round them.'

'Do you think so?'

'Yes. Go on. Have a try.'

'I say. What are you doing with that half-crown? Do you want to toss me double or quits?'

'No. That is, I . . .' I blushed and put down the coin on my bedside table. It was useless to attempt to bribe her.

'Well. I'll go and find my husband.'

'Does your husband live here?'

'Yes.'

Perhaps a waiter, I thought. At once I saw another avenue of attack.

'Don't you think he'd get me something to eat?'

'I shouldn't'—she answered, standing up and swaying again slightly—'say it was awfully probable.'

He was not a waiter then; possibly merely a boots. I decided to try once more, adopting the sort of bantering tone which she herself was using.

'I'm sure you can do something for me. I should think you get on pretty well with some of the waiters.'

'What,' she asked, slightly raising her eyebrows, 'makes you think that?'

It was against my principles, but I was compelled to flatter her.

'Well, you're very pretty.'

She moved slowly towards me. I have to admit that I smelt whisky on her breath. She took hold of my bedclothes and tucked them neatly under my chin. Then she turned out my bedside lamp, put my *Kinema Arts* on my side-table and said, quite distinctly:

> "Gentle Jesus, meek and mild,
> Blessings on this little child."

The light from the passage flashed into my room as she drifted through the door.

I lay quite still, staring at the ceiling, until worn out with hunger and travelling I fell asleep. And in my dreams that rather long, wistful, childish face hung always in front of me, filling me on that night, as on every night since, with the same feverish excitement composed, in almost equal parts, of melancholy and hope.

II

The Scriptwriter

VERY EARLY the next morning—it felt only an hour or two since I had gone to bed—I heard, as in a dream, a curious activity in the hotel. There was a good deal of shouting in the passages, sounds as of heavy machinery being dragged along, oaths, screams and scuffles, and out in the road a number of lorries seemed to be started with difficulty. I was too dazed to wonder much at this commotion and fell asleep again, not waking properly until almost eleven o'clock. Then I dressed hurriedly and went downstairs.

First of all I wanted to get hold of the director, for it was to him that the letter had been written which had got me into the unit. From what Mrs. Cooper had told me the night before, I realized that he must be the man my mother had known at the Art School, and I thought that this would be a good basis for my introduction. Failing him, I had decided to accost anyone in dark glasses and of a sufficiently eccentric appearance. But once more I saw no sign of the film people, and I decided to risk my reputation by enquiring for them at the reception desk.

'No, sir, it's quite all right. We've seen no sign of them to-day,' said the receptionist, and I was just turning away when I was addressed by a man who had been standing by the letter rack. If he wasn't a man for whom I later came to have a certain respect, I should have said he was reading other people's postcards.

'Looking for the Film Unit?' he asked.

'Why, yes. Do you happen to know where they are?'

'What are you, an extra?'

He pronounced this last word with such biting scorn that I
resolved, whatever an extra might be, not to be one.

'No. As a matter of fact I have just got a job with them.
I'm to be assistant to the director.'

At this he gave me a look of compassion and took my arm.

'You will have just arrived?'

'Yesterday.'

'Then you won't have played pontoon with Sparks or bar
billiards with Doris or gone drinking with Angela.'

I admitted to having had none of those pleasures.

'You will still, in fact, have some money in your pocket?'

'A little.'

'Then, as it is eleven o'clock, we will go out to coffee.'

He went to fetch a very dirty army mackintosh and a grey
cloth cap, and we set out together through the rain. As we
walked I looked at him and wondered how he could possibly
have anything to do with films. With his thin, sandy moustache
and close-cropped hair he looked like a retired military man of
just under middle age. He walked self-consciously, like a
soldier, and with a slight limp. Only his voice was out of
place, the thin, fastidious voice of a parson or a schoolmaster,
very affirmative in its high notes. I was still hungry and glad
when we arrived at the A.B.C. Since I had had no breakfast
I was not ashamed of my appetite. My companion, in any
case, would have put me at my ease at once by ordering baked
beans and a sardine salad and setting to as if he hadn't eaten
for a week. Not until his third cup of coffee had arrived did
he start to talk.

'Pelting,' he said with great satisfaction, looking at the rain
outside the A.B.C. windows. 'Pelting. And they've been trying to shoot since six o'clock. Just like Doris to call them all
for a day like this. The bitch!'

'Excuse me,' I said. 'You are in the Film Unit then?'

'Yes,' he said. 'That's right.'

'Yet you're not out 'with them to-day?'

'Oh no. He doesn't need a scriptwriter when he's shooting. A scriptwriter would only be in the way. He might want him to shoot something connected with the story.'

'You're a scriptwriter, then?' I looked at him with added respect. 'That must be very interesting. I've often wondered how one becomes a scriptwriter.'

'When I was a young man', the scriptwriter started when the waitress had brought him another plum flan, 'I was intended by my father for the army. I was sent to a Military College where I spent what now seem the happiest days of my life. I was young. I still had a sense of personal cleanliness and decency. I was surrounded by friends whose conduct was affected by considerations of good manners and honourable dealing. The life was extremely healthy and the meals regular. At that time I made the acquaintance of women with whom sexual intercourse was not to be had for the asking, and men who could hold their liquor. My servant cared for and respected me, and I didn't treat him entirely as a comic character. I could distinguish an insult from a civil remark, a brave man from a coward, and a French claret from an Australian. My conversation was not unsuitable for mixed company, and I flatter myself I could have ornamented some minor garrison post in Assam with competence and discretion. It was not to be.

'Once a year it was the custom of the cadets to present a sort of theatrical entertainment before dispersing for the Christmas vacation. These entertainments I, with natural good taste, had always found rather embarrassing than anything else. The better-looking boys dressed as women, and I had noticed that those who shone most on the stage were not always those who passed out first in the Lewis gun or received commissions in

the Brigade of Guards. Nevertheless, I was once tempted by a
friend to write a short piece for one of these occasions. He
was a man I was anxious to impress and, in an evil moment, I
agreed to do it.

'I was not uneducated, nor I flatter myself, stupid. I wrote
from the best models. I was as familiar with Molière and
Terence as I was with Johnson, Wycherley and Goldoni.
What I wrote was entertaining and well constructed. It suited
admirably the brusque, masculine occasion for which it was
designed. But it was not until I saw my piece performed that
I realized the enormity of what I had done.

'My play ended with the reconciliation of two friends who
had been rivals for the favour of a worthless woman. After a
comic duel they both reject her and she, leaving them in a
public park, engages the attention of two other young officers
just as, in the opening scene, she had met our friends. The dis-
illusioned suitors wonder whether to warn her new victims;
but decide not to. They have, after all, gone through a unique
and exciting experience which, for all its misery, they would
not have missed. Arm in arm they go off singing, pausing to
whisper a word of encouragement into the ears of their suc-
cessors. As I watched that on the stage, heard the fine tenor
voices and saw the curtain close with a decisive flourish over
the situation I had created, I had the ghastly feeling of having
contrived something beautiful. Had I only been brought up in
a less tolerant Anglicanism, been more deeply impressed, from
my youth, with a consciousness of sin, I might still have
avoided the error into which I then fell. I might have presented
my small library to my batman, burned my manuscript books
in the fire and gone away for a month's hunting to friends in
Northern Ireland. As it was I told both my father and my
colonel that I wished to write. For various reasons they made
no objection. My father loved me dearly and made great
personal sacrifices to support me until I should become estab-

lished. That never, in his lifetime, occurred: nor, to my own satisfaction, has it yet.

'I am now what is known as a professional writer. That is to say, I am a man of weak habits, uncertain substance, and undesirable acquaintance. I have even lost the courtesy to ask whether I am not boring you intolerably.'

As a matter of fact he was. I was anxious to hear about the Film Unit and was impatient of these reminiscences, the tone of which I then felt to be heretical. I protested politely, however, and the scriptwriter, after asking me for a cigarette, went on.

'In those days it was considered necessary for a young man starting out on a literary career to inhabit a certain part of London much frequented by whores, bedbugs and professional boxers. Nothing could be less conducive to composition. In fact, most of the day has to be spent in public houses to escape the extremely depressing atmosphere of the district. The drinking of much bitter beer undermines the health. The strain of the amorous affairs in which one is expected to engage ruins the nerve. Within a year I was incapable of writing a coherent sentence or reading anything more involved than the crime reports in the Sunday Press. None too soon I moved to furnished rooms in Wimbledon.

'There, in time, a little of my former lucidity returned. I wrote several plays, all of which were rejected by London managements. In time I should have certainly gone back to the army, if necessary to the ranks. But my misfortunes dogged me. One of my plays was put on by a Sunday society in Wimbledon and achieved a certain success. I watched it in terror. I saw as on the racecourse, the hurdles, the water jump, the fence on the corner which might have laid me low. And I saw myself triumphantly clear them. There was no question of construction that play set itself which I hadn't solved. My ingenuity was quite horrible.

'The next day I went for my usual morning walk on Wimbledon Common. In a secluded spot I fixed my ace of spades to a tree: I had always kept up revolver practice. Believe me I was still trembling so that I barely tipped the edge of the card. I, who had dreamed of an Indian garrison, was no longer fit to be brothel sergeant in Port Said.'

'And then,' I interrupted him, hoping to bring his interminable monologue round to the Film Unit again, 'you decided to write for the films?'

'You are a little previous,' he answered, 'with the final humiliation; but indeed it came soon enough. I have few needs, food and clean shelter are about all I ask. After my father died and my mother was provided for, I really had not enough to keep alive. I might, of course, have found honest employment at any labour exchange; but there was the temptation of being paid for actually writing. The producer of my play had joined a film company. I went with him.'

'I should have thought'—it was the sort of stupid remark I hope I now manage to avoid making—'there was a good deal of scope in writing for the films.'

'Scope,' he answered contemptuously, 'was the very word with which I drugged myself. I thought of the cinema as a revival of the popular tradition of the Elizabethan stage. I saw myself as one of the sixteenth-century Cambridge dramatists with a new medium and the whole world at my feet. And yet I knew in my heart that what a writer needs is not scope; but a strict limitation.'

He relit his cigarette, which had gone out, and sat staring at his empty coffee cup.

'But surely'; he looked so dejected that I had to say something, however fatuously, encouraging. 'Surely there are some opportunities . . .'

'Oh, yes. Occasionally a situation comes out as you've planned it. And the money is generous. And one gets expenses.

'Expenses?' I asked hopefully glancing at our rather large chit.

'Yes. To-day, for instance, I shall charge in two pounds for taking you out to lunch. It's a useful addition. Of course, I send fifty per cent of it to my mother.'

As I was paying his bill under such profitable circumstances to his family I felt justified in pressing him for more information.

'I don't know anything about the set-up down here,' I said. 'Is the Unit large?'

'Large enough. There's the cameraman, Sparks Henry. Comes, I believe, from the North. He's a genius at his work, but for all other purposes subhuman. Crankshott's the sound man—quite efficient. The continuity girl's called Daisy, a most astute young lady of whom you should beware. Then there are the other assistant directors, they do most of the work. Carpenters, electricians, a driver who should be under restraint. Oh, and Doris, the Unit manager. She's in charge of all the organization. She's . . .' he seemed to be searching for a word.

'What?' I asked.

'A bitch,' he said cheerfully.

'And the director?'

'And the director.'

'I've never met him. My mother knew him quite well.'

'You'll meet him in time, I expect. Only I shouldn't remind him of your mother. He's a man with a short memory.'

'He's very clever, isn't he?'

'He also is a genius at his work—and in no other respect subhuman.' And he seemed to mutter, 'Inhuman, perhaps.'

'Is that all?'

'Yes. Oh, the director's wife, of course. She goes everywhere with him. Quite a good Unit really,' he went on hurriedly. 'Riddled with intrigue, of course, but efficient at their work. It's a pity our contacts aren't equally efficient.'

'Contacts?'

'Yes, the soldiers we are filming. I tell you the organization of the army nowadays is amateurish compared with ours.'

I felt I should try and start work that afternoon, but the scriptwriter said 'No'.

'I expect you'll meet Doris and the other assistants this evening. Hang about the Red Lion, they'll probably be in about six o'clock. Doris is a bitch,' he repeated. And then, as we went out past a poster for the film I had seen the night before he asked: 'How many times have you seen that inconsistent bit of nonsense?'

'Only once,' I answered, surprised. 'How many have you?'

'Eleven. I'll complete my dozen with you.'

We spent the afternoon in the cinema. I couldn't be certain that the scriptwriter sat beside me weeping.

III

The Unit

W HEN WE came out of the cinema the scriptwriter gave
me a clear if not sympathetic description of the people I was
to look out for in the Red Lion. Then he gazed up at the
sky.

'Weather's clearing. I bet Doris is bringing them back now.
Just when they'd be able to start shooting. Serve her right.
The bitch.'

A pale sun appeared over the clouds like an invalid sitting
up in bed.

'Well, I think I'll go and put in a little clock golf. It's the
only exercise I get now. Thanks for the cinema.'

He limped cheerfully off down the steaming promenade
and I made for the Red Lion. I had by now identified the girl
in the film with my visitor of the night before; but the appearance of the real girl seemed so improbable that I was now half-
ready to believe I had seen the whole incident on the screen.
Thinking about it, however, brought me into the same excited
and bewildered state that I had been in the afternoon before,
and in that condition I arrived at the Red Lion, an ostentatious
and extremely well-supplied pub near to the railway station.
There, while I was waiting, I drank a Worthington. This
reminded me of my father and the evenings in which we
would sit together and he would drink, with the severe air
of one who knows how to make of bottled beer a servant
rather than a master, his single Worthington before bed.
Perhaps it was owing to his influence that I never got drunk

while I was on the location; although I may say I had every encouragement. The drinking habits of the Unit were peculiar for, while they spent every free moment in the pub, they were always ready for work in icy and almost terrifying sobriety. I make the point about my own moderation to assure the reader that however fantastic the following account may become, it is merely a direct, and as far as I could make it, lucid statement of the facts.

I hadn't been waiting long before there was a screeching of brakes in the road outside, several women ran into doorways or lay down on the pavement, and a van drew up to the curb. A remarkable procession entered. It was headed by a woman, Doris, I had no doubt, of quite embarrassing ugliness. She wore grey flannel trousers and a fur coat; from her lake lips dangled a short cheroot. She was of indeterminable age, though certainly over forty. I say her ugliness was embarrassing because there was a flagrancy about it, like great beauty it was offered provocatively, even underlined by harsh make-up and swept-back hair. She moved very well, regally and barbarically, and the train of young men behind her shuffled and cowered like henchmen. They were unremarkable young men, I counted four or five of them, one had hennaed hair and another was very young. They all seemed to have been to the same tailors, a firm which specialized in making rough jackets from travelling rugs. Behind them walked a plump girl in trousers carrying a thermos flask and a portable type-writer. The rear was brought up by the driver of the van, a creature whose appearance I can only describe as Neanderthal. I still can't believe it is possible for knuckles to hang so near to the ground.

When they were all in the pub they stood motionless before the bar, eyeing each other. This was no scene of reckless hospitality. How long their thirst and parsimony would have been balanced I have no idea. Driven on by a mad ambition to start my job I asked their leader, the woman, if she by any chance belonged to the Action Film Unit.

'Gin,' she answered gruffly.

'Gin.'

'Gin.'

'Gin.'

'Gin.'

'Gin and lime,' said the plump girl, truculently.

'*Crême de Menthe*,' added the Neanderthal man in a low, threatening tone.

Fortunately my mother had given me a pound to buy an extra shirt. I now had one-and-threepence change.

They shot their drinks back and stood looking at their empty glasses. The very young boy flushed deeply.

'I've been sent out to join them and I haven't been able to find them yet.'

Doris looked me up and down.

'Are you the new assistant director?'

I admitted it.

'I'm Doris,' she said, 'Unit manager. This is Bert, the first assistant, Harold the second, Fennimore the third, and Dorcas the fourth. You'll be the fifth. Another large gin please, miss. I suppose you'll all drink beer?'

She frowned round at her followers, who agreed.

'I won't have another one, thank you.'

'Yes, you will.'

'No, thank you.'

'What's the matter? Stomach trouble?'

'No. I never drink more than one, thank you all the same.'

'I'm paying.'

'Yes. Thank you. But I've had enough.'

'Bloody odd. Oh, I forgot, this is Daisy, the continuity girl, and Art Hepplethwaite, the driver. Bert, did you get Sparks and the camera assistants off on the other van?'

'Yes, Doris.' The first assistant fell out of the ranks to answer her. He was older than the rest, although his clothes were still the clothes of a young man. He looked terribly tired.

'How did the hourly boys get back?'

'I sent them by 'bus.'

'They didn't like that, did they?'

'They didn't mind. They'll all charge in for taxis.'

'Well,' Doris turned back to me, 'who do you know in the unit?'

'I've met the scriptwriter.'

'What was he doing, playing clock golf?' She said this so brutally that I couldn't laugh with my four colleagues and Art. I was pleased to notice that the continuity girl didn't laugh either; but gazed soulfully into her light ale.

'That man never does any work,' she went on, 'I want to get him fired.'

'Good idea,' said Fennimore.

'And you, too, if you can't keep those seagulls away from the camera,' she added darkly. Everyone else laughed and Fennimore smirked miserably. During my long and often terrifying acquaintance with Doris, this was the only sort of joking of which I found her capable. At first I supposed her threats were meant humorously and without malice; later I was to find out how mistaken I was.

At that moment Dorcas, in a hysterical effort to prevent this distressing badinage being directed at him, bought another round of drinks. When I refused he looked at me with bewildered gratitude. This time Art had Green Chartreuse.

'And what do you know about films?' Doris asked.

'I have a great belief in the cinema. I don't know much about the technical side yet. I hope to learn.'

'An arty type,' said Harold.

Even Doris laughed.

Encouraged by this success Harold bought a round of

drinks. Fennimore put his arm round the continuity girl's waist and Art went on to Kummel.

'Who got you into the unit?' Doris asked again, even more aggressively.

'My mother knew the director once.' I looked straight at her. 'She wrote to him.'

It had its effect. Doris remained silent.

I felt like a lion tamer who has at last found the whip crack which will subdue the most ferocious of his big cats. I was so elated I would have bought them all a round of drinks if the director's name had not induced a sudden fit of generosity in Bert. I was not sorry when I heard Art ask the manager to bring up a bottle of Benedictine.

'Well, you must be able to do something,' Doris admitted grudgingly. 'The director wouldn't take on an amateur. He's too good an organizer for that.'

'The greatest organizer in the world,' said Dorcas enthusiastically, raising his glass to the light.

'Shut up, you bloody little fool,' Doris sounded almost kindly. 'Art! Why the hell haven't you bought your round yet?'

'Hold your water,' Art replied graciously. 'Now, what are you all having? I'm for a nice glass of beer.' He lugged from his hip pocket a thick roll of pound notes, held together with an elastic female garter.

'Gin,' Doris rapped out.

'Gin.'

'Gin.'

'Gin.'

'Gin.'

'Gin and lime.'

'No thank you, really.'

'Good lad. Good-mannered lad, that.'

After the next round Doris looked at her wrist-watch.

'Time for one more round. And you can all damn' well buy your own.'

'No,' said Daisy with drunken abandon. 'My round.'

'I could fancy,' Art brought round a hand, from a surprisingly long distance, to scratch the back of his head, 'a drop of that Drambuie.'

'No, but he is the greatest organizer in the whole world,' said Dorcas and collapsed on to the floor.

'Time to go.'

They walked out over his body. As she herded them out Doris shouted back to me.

'You. Fifth assistant. Get Dorcas back to the hotel. Any time before six o'clock to-morrow morning. Oh, and get me twenty cigarettes.'

I realize now that I should have saved myself a great deal of future trouble if I had then spat in her eye. I was not, at that time, ready with that sort of gesture and so I stayed where I was. I was not certain, as I saw Art lurch into the driving seat, that I had not chosen wisely. As the van drove off I heard a woman screaming up the street and little Dorcas, gripping my leg, groaned faintly. A taxi happened to be passing and, with my last one-and-threepence I had him conveyed back to the hotel.

IV

An Assistant Director

WHEN I STAGGERED into the hotel lounge, supporting Dorcas with one arm round his waist, the Film Unit had again disappeared. The lounge was shrouded in early evening shadows, from which Mrs. Cooper rose gracefully and advanced towards us.

'Oh dear. Is your friend not feeling well?'

'A touch,' I said, with hopeless lack of conviction, 'of the sun.'

She produced a large silver bottle of smelling-salts and waved it under the boy's nose.

'Christ! Stink of cats!'

Before he should further disgrace himself I hurried him to the lift.

'Caught up,' the liftman asked gloatingly, 'in the sickening round of pleasure?'

I held Dorcas in both arms and assented.

'Them picture people. Life is a giddy whirl for them.'

He stopped the lift suddenly and Dorcas fell out.

As we blundered along the passage we heard the roar of taps from behind a door and the voice of a girl singing. I don't think I have ever heard a cheap American song given such a delicious thrill of enjoyment. We both stopped.

'The lovely wife,' said Dorcas, 'of the greatest organizer in the world, singing in her bath.'

And, throwing himself at the locked door, he rattled the handle violently.

'Fire! Fire! Fire! Let me in at once.'

'Good boys. Go to bed,' a cool voice answered from inside, the voice that had been sounding in my ears all day. But I had no time to think over this latest discovery. My immediate concern was to get Dorcas into my room and lay him down.

I achieved this with a little difficulty. When he was stretched out on my pink satin counterpane I remembered a remedy for drunkenness which always appears sovereign in films. An ewer of water is dashed into the face of the sufferer. My annoyance with Dorcas made me inclined to try this violent expedient, and it had the most sobering effect on him. Unfortunately it also drenched my bed and I spent the next three nights in an armchair.

Dorcas blinked, coughed, and then sat up and looked at me.

'Well,' he said, in a rather arrogant voice, 'it will be nice to have an assistant.'

I sat down on a chair beside him. This was obviously the time for me to find out my exact position in the unit.

'I came down here,' I said, 'as assistant to the director.'

Dorcas looked worried.

'Don't you understand,' he said, 'that it takes about twenty years to become a first assistant director?'

'Then how old,' I asked naïvely, 'must the director be?'

'I don't know.' Dorcas lay back. 'I haven't seen him yet.'

'You haven't seen him?'

'Of course not. We haven't had any weather. Don't you know anything about our work here?'

I confessed my ignorance.

Dorcas propped himself up on my pillow and lit a small Turkish cigarette. Pale as his shirt he looked like a very young soldier who had been wounded in battle. However, any pity I might have felt for him was dispelled by the unbearably superior manner with which he treated me. I hope I should have been able to forgive that if I had known then the humiliations which he himself must have gone through as the youngest assistant on the unit.

'We've been down here about two months. Trying to shoot a film about the army training. Of course, the scriptwriter has cooked up some sort of a story to keep the producers quiet . . .'

He rapped this introduction out as if it was the minimum of information he must give me before he started issuing orders.

'. . . But we're not taking any notice of that. Just now we're covering general action stuff. The weather has been against us, so after Doris has chosen the location and Bert has got the camera set up and Harold has called the soldiers and Fennimore has arranged for tea to be brought out on the cliffs, the rain has usually settled in for the day and so it isn't worth calling the director.'

'And what do you do?' I asked him.

'Oh. I dirty the soldiers' faces or give them signals. Up till now I've had to carry the tea-urn up the cliffs; but since you've come I won't have to do that any more.'

I didn't like the turn the conversation was taking.

'Does all this,' I said, 'give you a very valuable training for films?'

I doubt whether Dorcas had ever had time to think of it in this light. However, he was quick with his reply:

'Look here. I used to work in the office in London. That was very interesting, of course, but we all wanted to get on the production side. Well, I was lucky. Doris needed someone to carry her luggage to the station and I carried it right on to the train and sat on it and got brought down here by mistake. Well, I worked my way up and now she actually knows my name and gives me an assistant director's work to do. (Although for some reason they still pay me as an office boy.) I mean to go on working until my chance comes.'

'Your chance?' I asked.

'Yes. All assistant directors get a chance some time. If you're always on time and do everything you're asked to do twice as quickly as Harold or Fennimore could do it, then one day Bert might crack up (he's been to the doctor twice already about his insomnia), and they might let you rehearse the soldiers for a small scene (one that they don't think will be left in the picture) or say "Quiet please" before the director says "Action". Then if you're a good first assistant, you're worth twenty pounds a week to any studio.'

I suppose I still looked dubious, for Dorcas went on quickly:

'But anyway, you've got to start at the bottom and get kicked around a bit. You'll never appreciate the organization if you don't. Believe me, my lad, films are all a matter of organization: organization and discipline. Of course, we don't do much organization to begin with, just arrange for meals and rooms and so on.'

'Who's the chief organizer then?' I asked.

'Some people think it's Bert, but Doris has got him taped. He's like a child in her hands. It's my belief she knows something about his private life.'

'So Doris is the real head of the unit?' I asked, in some dismay.

'You might think so,' said Dorcas mysteriously, 'but you'd be wrong. I don't believe Doris can move an inch without the director's permission. And there is no point of organization ever so small, but the director himself has a hand in it. Just to give you an instance: the director's wife sometimes comes out on location with us; she knows how the director will want things if the weather clears. Well, one day when I went to get the tea I told the old girl in the shop that we should need an extra slice of cake. Can you believe it: she knew already! The director had 'phoned up in the afternoon and warned her. That just sums up his eye for detail.'

'I should have thought that the director would have been too concerned with artistic problems . . .'

Dorcas turned and looked at me with almost kindly contempt.

'Would you like a word of advice?' he asked.

I nodded obediently.

'Then stop using that word "artistic". It'll only make Bert lose his temper.'

'But why . . . ?'

'Bert's horrible when he loses his temper. I think it must be something to do with his never going to sleep.'

So for the last time I was choked off any serious talk about films. After that I used sometimes to discuss the cinema with the boot-boy at the hotel who kept a small Kodak projector in his cupboard. On this we showed each other the *Cabinet of Doctor Caligari*, and on my advice he took out a year's subscription to *Kinema Arts*.

Dorcas was obviously a great deal more interested in the organization of the unit than in the films they were going to produce, so I went on to question him further on the subject. I got the impression of a relentless efficiency kept alive by the most merciless intrigue.

'The scriptwriter told me to beware of Daisy,' I said.

'Daisy's jolly loyal to the unit,' Dorcas replied. 'She used to be a bit sweet on the scriptwriter, only she soon found out he wasn't really keen on his job. Takes too long to get out of bed in the mornings for a real film type. So when she had to type out his scripts she altered them all hoping he'd get the sack. He would have if Doris hadn't shown her up—Doris knows that Daisy's after her job, and she wanted to get her in wrong with the director. But then Fennimore told them that Bert had called them the weird sisters in bed one night, and they both joined together to try and sack him. And now the script-writer has his manuscripts typed out by the director's wife.'

'Yes, the director's wife,' I said. 'What exactly is her job in the unit?' To my surprise I found myself trembling as I asked this question, and also to my surprise I saw Dorcas blush deeply.

'She goes everywhere with the director,' he answered shortly. 'She's the most delightful woman, of course; but I don't think she'd do very well in an executive job. Poor memory: always calls me Fennimore.'

At this Dorcas's young features hardened. He sat up straight on my bed and rapped out:

'Well, my lad. Better get some sleep. Six o'clock call to-morrow.'

Then he added, more apologetically:

'Funny the way that drink took me. Must have had a chill or something.'

He left hurriedly. In the passage I heard him break into a run.

I had just finished selecting the few dry blankets from the flood in my bed when there came a tap on my door and the scriptwriter entered furtively. He was wearing an old camel-hair dressing-gown and smoking a meerschaum pipe.

'Oh, good evening. Do you mind if I wait here a moment?'

'Not at all. I was just going to sleep, but . . .'

'Thank you.' He sat down at my dressing-table and surveyed the wreckage.

'Had an accident?'

'Well, that is, I . . .'

'I hope,' he changed the subject before I could give my explanation, 'that you managed to find the unit.'

'Oh yes, I found them.'

He looked at me sympathetically. Then he produced a battered hip-pocket flask from his dressing-gown.

'Have a drink?'

'No, thank you.'

'May I borrow your tooth-glass?'

'Certainly.'

'Frightful, aren't they?'

'Well, I haven't known them very long.'

'Did you meet them all?'

'I don't think so. There's one person I still think I oughtt meet. After all, as I told you, my mother knew him well.'

'Who's that?'

'The director.'

'Yes. Perhaps you will meet him. You know, he's not the same, quite definitely not the same as the others. All of us, even I, respect him. But it's not him we keep in our thoughts as we raise our glasses to the light.'

As the scriptwriter squinted through my tooth-glass at the electric bulb it occurred to me for the first time that he, too, was a little drunk. Then I heard the sound of water running away and the slap of slippers in the passage. As if it were a signal the scriptwriter rose and made for the door:

'Sorry I couldn't stay longer,' he murmured, 'work. Work the most awful hours, you know, in the film business.'

V

The Director's Wife

I slept little enough that night, and I was awake well
before it was time to get up for the six o'clock call. By
the time I got downstairs, however, the Film Unit were already
assembled, standing like statues on the porch of the hotel,
motionless against the grey drizzle. As well as the group I had
met the evening before I noticed another set of people huddled
round a tripod and several large boxes. In the background
was a car, a sort of shooting-brake and a van at the wheel of
which I recognized the simian figure of the driver Hepplethwaite, muffled in a fur coat and wearing a black Homburg
hat.

'Damn nearly late,' said Doris. 'Tell him what to do Dorcas.'

Dorcas spoke. None of the others moved.

'Run upstairs and fetch the hourly boys.'

'What,' I asked as patiently as possible, 'are the hourly
boys?'

A cold gust of laughter blew amongst them. Then they
were all silent until Hepplethwaite answered from his van.

'Workmen. Carpenters, electricians, see? They get paid by
the hour instead of getting a weekly salary, see? Being older
men with families, they're not in the habit of getting up of a
morning like you lot, see? Now you've got to go and roust
them out.'

'See?' added a fat man who was standing by the tripod. He
wore a green pork-pie and spoke in a Yorkshire accent.

'Why the hell don't they send us someone who's trained?'

Bert demanded of the sky, and then fell to biting his finger-nails.

'Where,' I asked, 'are these men to be found?'

'Top floor, rooms 7, 8 and 9.'

I turned on my heel and re-entered the hotel.

'To bed late and up early,' said the liftman sententiously, 'burn the candle at both ends, you film people do.'

The top floor of the hotel seemed divided into a number of low attics. The first two of these, rooms 7 and 8, although containing three or four beds, were empty. From the third, number 9, a confused noise was issuing. I walked straight in and stood blinking on the threshold. The place was more like a bar than a bedroom. Round a table in the centre a dozen men were playing cards, all smoking heavily. They were in various stages of undress, some wore pyjamas, some long white suits of combinations, some trousers and vests; but all had kept on their hats. The various stools and chairs, even the shelves of the open wardrobe, were crowded with empty beer bottles.

I was considerably relieved that I shouldn't have to wake these men up.

'Here he is at last,' said one.

'Look, chum.' Another thrust a crumpled piece of paper under my nose. 'Doesn't this look like a two?'

'We've been up since two o'clock. Thought it was a two o'clock call.'

'I'm sorry,' I started, 'I hope you haven't been incon-venienced.'

'No, bless you boy, not at all.'

I thought this very civil of them.

'Of course, we'll be charging in for the four extra hours. Will that be all right?'

'I expect so,' I said thoughtlessly. 'Now, if you wouldn't mind coming downstairs they're all ready to start.'

'Certainly we're coming.'

'No trouble at all.'

'Bring the cards, Jim.'

'Just let me get my little chest-protector.'

'Lovely morning for an execution, eh?'

'Bleeding majesty getting restive, is she?'

'Bring your mouth-organ, Jim. And the cards.'

'You boys bringing plenty of books to read?'

They struggled into coats, gloves, scarves, mittens and overcoats.

'Are you all here?' I asked efficiently.

'All but the head electrician. He's motoring down from London; won't be here until mid-day,' I was told.

'Well, shall we go?'

As I shepherded them along the passage they went on babbling happily. An elderly man with a beard and a beret, who seemed to be their leader, skipped along beside me, looking up into my face and grinning in a friendly fashion.

'You a new one, are you?'

'Yes.'

'Oxford or Cambridge by any chance?'

'I'm afraid not.'

'Good. They never last long. Although Cambridge last longer than Oxford, I will say.'

We arrived at the head of the stairs. We all stood still and looked at the lift.

'Oo!' said a tall emaciated man in the background. 'The Cage of Death.'

'We walk,' said the bearded man. 'My boys want danger money to go down that one.'

We started the descent.

'She made a jump for you yet?' he asked.

'Who?'

'Her majesty. Queen of Sheba. Bleeding Doris.'

'Of course not.'

'You mind out. Get ready to duck. She's been after Soapy, hasn't she, Soapy?'

'Oh, don't talk so soft,' said the thin man coyly.

We descended another flight. Sleepy chambermaids and guests on the way to the bathroom viewed our procession with concern.

'You new to the business?'

'Yes.'

'I been in it thirty-one years. I was a star, you know, in the silent days. Henry Irving, Fatty Arbuckle, they were all "old boy" to me.'

'Good heavens!'

In the hall they broke into a run at the sight of Doris and crowded into the van. When they were all settled comfortably and had got their cards out, it was obvious there would be no room for me. I went round to the front.

'No room here, boy,' said Art. 'This is where Doris is riding.'

The shooting-brake was already crowded by the five assistants, the camera gear and its attendants.

'Thou'lt have to pad the hoof,' said the man in the porkpie hat, whom I found at the wheel.

'That's all right, Sparks,' said Doris, who came up biting the end off her first cheroot. 'He can go by 'bus.'

'I'll take him.'

The voice came from the depths of the long, black car. A door opened and I found myself enveloped in grey upholstery, breathing perfume, incidentally touching fur.

'The poor, hungry boy.'

To my confusion I recognized the visitor I had so stupidly taken for a chambermaid.

'Are they still underfeeding you?'

'No. That is, yes. But . . .'

She raced the engine and the car leapt off. At a particularly
nasty corner she took her hand off the wheel and opened a
pigeon-hole on the dashboard. It was full of sandwiches.

'They're lovely,' she said. 'Give yourself a treat.'

'No, really.'

'Go on. Why will these pedestrians jump about so?'

'Thank you very much then.'

'Not at all. Growing lad and all that.' She leant forward
and squinted through the windscreen. 'I ought really to wear
my glasses for this, only they do make one so hellishly ugly.'
We stopped at some lights. 'I wonder what gear this is?'

It was reverse. Fortunately the cyclist behind saw us coming.

'Are you the new assistant, then?'

'Yes.' I asked nervously: 'Your husband's the director, isn't
he?'

'That's right. You ought to meet him. He eats a lot, too.'

We slithered round a corner and started to mount the road
to the cliffs.

'I should like to get to know him. He won't be out to-day,
will he?'

'No. He's planning the film back at the hotel. He says the
really important shooting won't start until the operation
begins. He'd like to try and get the army to put off the
operation until summer.'

'Operation?' I asked.

'Yes. Of course, I suppose I shouldn't really be talking
about it. Damn, I never mean to miss that turning. It always
seems camouflaged somehow.'

The caravan behind us had turned off, while we went
bounding on into the countryside.

'Still, I'm sure if we keep turning to the—what a peculiar
noise—right it'll come to the same thing in the end.'

It didn't come to the same thing. It came to a stretch of
deserted downland on which no habitation or living thing

was to be seen. Undiscouraged, the director's wife turned to the right. We bumped along a bridle track until we arrived at a square white building, a sort of primitive inn.

'Let's stop here and ask someone. Shall I draw into this gateway?'

She drew into it. There was a sickening crash and a man with a thick belt came up waving his fist.

'Criminals,' he cried. 'Lunatics. Thoughtless hogs to rush around destroying poor people's homes.'

'Oh dear,' said the director's wife. 'So inconvenient. And now everyone's going to get furious.'

'What they've saved up for,' the man went on, 'with the labour of a life time.'

But she advanced on him with such a compelling smile, looked so helpless and tragic and anxious to make amends that he soon softened, offered to ring up the garage and even, seeing it was so early in the morning, invited us into his sitting-room to warm up and have a bite of breakfast.

During this time the director's wife behaved with such flagrant charm that even I was a little shocked. I am convinced, however, that although she realized her good manners were quite artificial, she exhibited them with the best intentions, meaning them as honest payment for the broken gate-post and the bacon and fried tomato. Whatever her real state of mind, and I am only guessing at it now and certainly couldn't have attempted to guess at it then, she quite satisfied the inn-keeper, who opened the bar for us immediately after breakfast.

As I sat over my Worthington and the director's wife— Angela, as she herself asked me to call her—bought her second whisky, I felt the day was not to be quite a misery after all. The rain had thickened, there was no sign of the breakdown van, only a sort of pricking conscience about my work (an early inheritance, I am inclined to think, from my father) spoiled my complete enjoyment.

'My poor sweet,' said Angela. 'You can't walk over there, and the weather will prevent them shooting anyway.'

'I shouldn't think anything will prevent them having tea.'

'Oh, Dorcas can do that. He's done it for the last three weeks. You haven't got anything to worry about. It's I that's got to do the worrying. He's going to be livid.'

I knew at once whom she referred to as, almost proudly, she breathed the last sentence. We both sat in silence, thinking of the same man, and I must have spoken my thought, without realizing it.

'Is he, then, so very frightening?'

She answered beneath her breath, as if her thoughts were speaking for her too.

'They're all scared of him, of course. Scared of what he'll do, what he'll say. I'm only scared in the way that, sometimes, I get scared of myself.'

She went to the bar and flashed her carefully regulated smile.

'Can you spare another whisky?'

As she walked back she was looking thoughtful.

'Still, marriage is awfully difficult, don't you think? You've met the scriptwriter? He seems to understand everything about it, and he's very sweet too. Sometimes I don't think my husband understands anything about it all. When you meet him you must tell me what you think about him.'

As I certainly didn't intend to make a judgment on the director, even when I knew him, I remained silent.

'The way I first met him was really rather funny . . .' Angela began. Then she looked round and the innkeeper brought the bottle and the syphon over to our table.

Although the three members of the Film Unit who spoke to me intimately at this time were all, in a measure, drunk, they were so dissimilar in their manner that I must draw some distinction between them. Dorcas's drunkenness increased his effort at self-discipline, made him brusque and aggressive; a young officer suffering from a stammer who still has to command his men. The scriptwriter, for the short time I had seen him, had been even more courteous, more kindly, in his cups. He seemed mellowed, wiser, aged even as if drink had the same effect as many years spent in solitude and contemplation. And Angela? Of her I cannot speak with so much definition, for I am not sure if the greater intoxication was hers or mine. Only I can say that in the following account her speech was more lyrical, more high and sweet and arrogant than I had heard it; that her words, although her syntax occasionally became confused, seemed to sing and echo with meaning; and that her voice broke bravely round me like the ring of a wine-glass, or the distant cry of a hunting-horn through iced woods in winter.

'You know, as a girl, I was really quite nicely brought up,' she began, after she had lit a cigarette.

'I lived with my father in the lodge of his country house, Bluewater. I think my great-grandmother was the last one of our family who had actually lived in the house itself. It was a fantastic place, with a maze and a Chinese pavilion and ceilings painted by someone during the Restoration who was supposed to be rather good. I had never seen the house lived in, but I wandered about there a lot when I was a little girl. I was always sliding down the marble banisters, and bathing in the lily-pond and rowing on the lake, and getting lost in the maze and talking to a statue in the garden called "Priapus". The garden was full of statues, soldiers with greaves and breast-plates and warts and periwigs, slim boys of bronze, and pale, stone girls who looked down and sheltered their stomachs with their hands. I remember dolphins and cherubs round the fountains and brazen lions at the gates. I had lots of time to look at all these things; I don't believe I ever played with other children.

'In the evenings I used to go back to the lodge and play draughts with my father. My father was a great believer in what he called "silent companionship", which was convenient because it meant neither of us had to talk at all. He was very fond of fishing, and the lodge was always cluttered up with waders and old mackintoshes and rods and tweed hats with hooks in them. All our meals were trout or pike, roach or even eels, and sometimes salmon when he went away to Devonshire.

'Although he never said much to me, I think he missed me when I went away to school, and was glad when I came back for the holidays. I expect he misses me now, because I never go home at all.

'It's funny. I went to an awfully respectable school. In the evenings the mistresses wore gowns from Molyneux and the sixth-form girls learnt Italian. No old girl would have dared to come back for a visit if she hadn't been presented at Court. I learnt some things there which were awfully useful. You see, I used to steal rather a lot when I was young, and there they taught me not to.

'When I came back from school I was bored at first. I missed lacrosse and netball and trips up to London to matinées with the English mistress, who was rather charming as a matter of fact. Then during my last term I had been a prefect and I missed that too. All the other girls I knew were coming out and having parties and so on, but there didn't seem much chance of a party at Bluewater, and my father never seemed to have the fare for me to go up to London.

'But, in a little while, I settled down. I spent all my time in the big house, dusting the rooms and putting flowers about in the vases, white porcelain, and cut-glass, and painted china, which I filled with roses and lilies, round sunflowers and trailing honeysuckle in season. Then I would go and lie on the grass. From one lawn your body would press out scents of thyme and rosemary, and dream of the rich, rather brutal middle-aged squire who would ride up across the paddock and marry me so we could live in Bluewater again. I always expected my husband to burst suddenly on me in the middle of that park and snatch me up in his arms and, in fact, that is almost what happened.

'One day my father, whom friends had taken away to fish in Devonshire, wrote to tell me that a film company who were making a film about English Architecture wanted to take some pictures of Bluewater. He had given them permission, and would I see, if they came when he was still away, that they got what they wanted? For some reason I was very angry about this, and when they arrived I sent the house-keeper to show them round. I spent the whole day in the lodge gazing resentfully at the stuffed pike on the wall. Ever since I remembered Bluewater had been empty, derelict, neglected by everyone except me. I was jealous of its new fame. Perhaps if the film company had come to photograph Miss Angela Upshott in her Carolean home in the country I should have felt differently. Do you see what I mean?

'I stayed in the lodge until evening, and then I walked across to the house to see if the film people had finished. It was a late summer evening, there were deep blue shadows under the yew hedges, behind "Priapus" and the warrior, and the water in the fountains was jet black. Only the hall of the house was lit with the garish crudity of arc lamps. I had never seen the chessboard paving so clearly or the elaborate celestial war-fare on the ceiling. The curtains looked threadbare and the staircase had lost all its mystery. The place looked both more artificial and less entrancing. I can't explain.'

'I think you're explaining awfully well,' I put in, en-raptured.

'It's only because I'm a bit tight. I don't usually talk so much as this, you know.'

'Do go on,' I said, 'if you don't mind.'

She puffed out a thin trumpet of smoke. Her eyes regained their detached expression.

'The camera was set up in the hall. There was no one there but the director. You'll be bound to meet him so I shan't try and describe him to you. I only say he's one of those people whose age it would be quite pointless to try and guess, and he looks now exactly as he did then. As I came up the stone steps, through the open double doors, he was lighting a cigarette. As he saw me he threw it away and started to . . .'

She paused for so long, searching for a word perhaps, or at last measuring the propriety of pouring out details of her past life to a strange youth in a public bar, that, overcome with curiosity, I ventured to interject.

'Started to?'

'To . . . to chase me.'

'Chase you?'

'Yes. That's exactly what he did. He started forward and I turned away. I walked more quickly and I heard him running. I ran as well. I ran as fast as I could, and since I came fresh from the lacrosse field and he was a man of . . . But there, I am still as much in the dark as ever, a man of thirty, forty, fifty, I wouldn't know. At any rate he was a man not fresh from the lacrosse field or any field at all, and his fastest was that much slower than mine. All the same, he gave me a race for, I suppose, my virginity. Down the drive and in and out the elm trees, up the rock garden and across the lawn, in between herbaceous borders, rose beds and cabbage beds, among cucumber frames and marrow hills, round statues, sundials, fountains and greenhouses, almost catching me up when I tripped on a watering can and fell, staining my dress green, almost losing me as I hid behind the potting shed and started out in the opposite direction, he kept up the chase in deathly silence, breathing heavily. On the bowling green I lost my shoe. On the paddock fence he tore his trousers. By the lily pond I dropped my bracelet, trying to delay him, but he didn't stop to pick it up. At last I lured him into the maze and we stumbled up the dark gravel paths, in between the wet hedges of privet. In the end I got ahead, crawled out of a gap I knew, and left him to blunder round on his own. I ran all the way home and sank down, exhausted, among the gum-boots and overcoats in the hall. I believe I went to sleep.'

Angela told this part of her story in a quick, hushed voice, panting a little as she spoke. When she had finished her account of this remarkable pursuit she calmed down and went on more naturally.

'I didn't see him again for almost six months. I had been up to London, on money some aunts had given me as a birthday present, to meet an old school friend. She was as poor as I was and she had got a job in an office. I envied her bed-sitting room with its telephone and gas-fire. As a matter of fact, I was beginning to get a bit bored in the country. Changing the flowers in Bluewater and reading the inscriptions on the sundials didn't excite me all that much any more. I was even beginning to find "Priapus" a little bit dreary and obscene. I told my father I was going to earn my living, and he said he thought it was a good idea and instead of having his latest five-pound roach stuffed he gave me the money for my fare back again and some jewellery of my mother's and a bag of biscuits in case I was hungry on the train. As I say, he really was rather sweet, and I've never seen him since.

'Well, then it all happened quite quickly. I went to an agency and the only people who wanted secretaries were the film people. I had an interview. I couldn't type or do short-hand, but it seemed to matter awfully little. At first I didn't connect them at all with the man who had chased me round Bluewater. Then, one day, he came into the office, and of course, neither of us mentioned it. I became his personal secretary. I can't imagine why I'm telling you all this.'

'Do you want to?' I asked. 'Please don't go on if you don't want to.'

'For some ghastly reason,' she said, 'I rather think I do. Just now I'm in a bit of a fix, and perhaps it'll help me to get it straightened out.'

'If I can be of any help . . .' At that moment I badly needed a second Worthington.

'Just then,' Angela went on, 'I was beginning to find my bed-sitting room a little grim. Each evening I'd get into pyjamas and squat in front of the gas-fire smoking cigarettes and wonder, if I died, how soon anyone would find out where I was. Certainly the director wouldn't have known, because at that time he treated me quite impersonally at the office. I had learnt typing and became quite a useful part of his ruthlessly efficient organization, and I don't think he thought of me as a human being at all. Certainly he never looked at me as he had that evening at Bluewater, nor did he make any advances. I will say that for him. He was different from Swartch and Underling, the producers; but that's another story.

'Well, as I say, I was getting rather bored in my room. So one evening I went to see the director. I had ready as an excuse that I wanted to bring him some scripts he had left in the office. He lived in a block of flats. His drawing-room had looking-glass on the walls, and white corduroy-covered furniture. There were no pictures, only stills from his films. The flowers were made of cellophane and wire. The clock had no numbers, only dots, and as I sat watching it, waiting for his valet to tell him I was there, I thought of the sundial at Bluewater and its inscription "Pereunt et Imputantur". At school I had been quite good at Latin.

'When he came in I said: "I should like to live here." '

'He looked at me. At Bluewater I had seen a sort of wild ambition in his eyes which terrified me. Now I only saw the most perfect self-confidence.

' "Why don't you?" he said.

' "All right," I said. "I will."

'Next week I wrote to my father. I told him: "I am living with a man in his flat. Would you much rather I was married to him, darling?"

'He wrote back and told me "Yes."

'So we were married the next week-end at a registry office in Maidenhead.

'I suppose I ought to tell you that he behaved rather badly after our marriage. Certainly he took no notice of me all day and often went out by himself at night. He is awfully selfish and has a beastly temper. At first he gave me parts in his films. I think I was quite a success; although I can't act at all, and I always used to be sick in end-of-term plays at school. I gave it up really because I was terrified of becoming too famous, more famous than he was, because I knew he wouldn't forgive me for that. Later on he started to take me out with him more. Then, when I stopped acting, he took me to the studio. But I knew I was only like his spaniel and whisky-flask and gold-mounted shooting-stick. A sort of mascot. Having me sitting by him in a deck-chair as he worked added to his power. Look, he felt people used to say, he's not only clever and commanding, but he's got himself a pretty wife. Am I being beastly about him?'

'No,' I protested, as if I'd have minded if she was.

'Because, you know, I can't honestly say I loved him any less. But love's so bloody tricky. Do you understand it?'

'No,' I swallowed. 'I can't say I do, completely.'

'I don't think the scriptwriter does, either. Although he understands practically everything else. How the director is to live with, for instance, and how he treats me, and never thinks of ordinary, decent things like how I have birthdays every year, or like going out to dinner and theatres and flowers and perhaps a cat.'

At that moment I could have challenged the director to a duel.

'Only why I talk so much about myself I can't imagine. But I've been thinking. Really now, it's come to the point of choosing between them . . .'

I gazed at her in silence, horrified by the gaping problem which she had opened before me. I couldn't think of the director, who seemed so remote and legendary to me, as involved in the ordinary tussle of emotions. I couldn't think of her made unhappy in this way. Finally, I was shocked by the behaviour of the scriptwriter which seemed to me questionable in the extreme. I was so distressed that I sat dumbly on, while she, apparently far less distressed than I, got up and smilingly stretched.

'Well, *you* couldn't care less. Let's play darts until the breakdown men come. And you shall talk about yourself. Only if you talk about your girl-friend in the A.T.S. I shall scream.'

I knew no one in the A.T.S. We played darts in silence.

Later we had lunch and went to sleep. The breakdown van didn't arrive until evening, then we were towed back to the town. Angela had a great bunch of daffodils presented her by the innkeeper, who assured her that the damage done to the gate was the merest bagatelle.

Angela was singing as we were towed past the Red Lion. The van and shooting-brake were outside, and we went in to meet the rest of the unit. I was a little nervous of my reception at first; but apparently the director's authority, vested in his wife, protected me. I was not even blamed by Dorcas, although I felt his hatred.

It didn't appear that they had had an altogether successful day. Apart from the rain the hourly boys had seemed to be suffering from a curious lassitude. They had kept on lying down to rest and were quite unable to work. Dorcas had slipped on the wet path up the cliffs and dropped the tea-urn into the sea, and Doris had caught a nasty cold. One of the soldiers had gone off with the camera in the lunch hour and taken pictures of girls in the tea room for a shilling a time. Finally, Art Hepplethwaite had surprised them all by driving the van suddenly away at mid-day and not reappearing with it until long after they wanted to go home. When it got back the inside of the van had apparently smelt strongly of fish.

Besides Doris had to complain of the attitude of the officers, which she said was becoming increasingly un-co-operative. She doubted if the bastards, as she called them, would consent to spend another day hanging about with painted faces in the rain with nothing to do. Worst of all, the captain had crept into Crankshott's sound van and record-ed a lot of limericks of his own composition about members of the Film Unit. But for timely action on Doris's part this sound-track would have been sent off and developed. She would like to have had him court-martialled.

After one drink Angela left for the hotel and asked me if I was coming with her. Of course I was. The car had gone on to the garage, so we walked down the promenade. As always in the evening, as if to taunt the Film Unit, the weather cleared. The sun reappeared just on that point of the smeared horizon where a small blue steamer passed hooting.

'How silly of me to bore you so to-day,' she said.

In the municipal gardens I saw a lonely figure discard his mackintosh before starting on another round of clock golf.

VI

The Soldiers and the Ping-pong Balls

By the end of the first week, although I had not yet met
the director, I had got a pretty good idea of the unit and of
the job they were doing. This job they thought enormously
important—and they spoke of the day when a few of them
were to go abroad to cover the actual front-line fighting as
if their expedition would be far more valuable to the war
effort than that of the soldiers themselves, whom they regarded
with more and more contempt. Indeed the army did seem to
have been doing all it could to delay the film. That the fighting
men should be so flippant about the whole business outraged
Doris and her assistants, and I think even the scriptwriter,
although he kept up his attitude of the innate decency of all
men of action as opposed to mere artists, was rather shocked.
I had no opportunity to judge between them until the end of
the week, because incessant rain kept us all in the hotel. The
day came, however, when I did go out to the location and
met the soldiers for the first time. These men were to play
such a large part in my story, and so to influence my attitude
to the Film Unit, that I think I must describe my first encounter with them in some detail.

The night before Doris had received a favourable weather
report from the Air Ministry. Our excitement had been enormous. The director had sent word that he had decided to use
the day, if it should indeed be fine, to shoot one of the most
important scenes in the film. Doris had worked incessantly
and dictated an enormous body of instructions on to Daisy's

54

typewriter. The call had been made for an hour earlier than usual. The night before no one had touched strong drink. All of us had learnt the call sheet by heart before sleeping.

Next morning, for once, we saw the cliffs clear of rain. The sun rose from the sea in a propitious haze. By the time that it was free to flood our scene the camera was set up, the reflectors in position, the microphone wired and Angela ready to drive back and fetch the director. Doris was walking about importantly with a script.

'In this scene we have the two officers and the sergeant with his platoon. Are the soldiers here?'

We all looked round. Over the whole length of the cliffs there was not a soldier in sight.

'Well, where the hell are they, Bert?'

'Yes, where are they, Harold?'

'Where are the soldiers, Fennimore?'

'Dorcas. Don't just stand there. Find out what's happened to them.'

'Why didn't you check up on the soldiers?'

'I never knew . . .' I said.

'It was your business to know.'

'Well, someone'd better get along to H.Q. and get them out before the director arrives,' said Doris.

'Get along to H.Q., Harold,' said Bert.

'And get the soldiers here, Fennimore.'

'Two officers and a platoon, Dorcas.'

'And run,' said Dorcas.

'Where is it?' I asked.

Dorcas pointed to a cluster of Nissen huts on a distant crag.

I left them, a group of tense, nervous figures, huddled round the expectant eye of their camera.

A quarter of an hour later I climbed over a stile into the army encampment. I was not challenged. I walked up to one of the huts and peered in at the door. The scene in the smoke-

laden atmosphere was identical to that which had met my
eyes when I had gone to call the hourly boys. After I had
explained my business one of the soldiers volunteered to take
me to see the captain. After some difficulty we found him in a
long hut; he was playing ping-pong which his major. Both
officers I recognized, the major from the hotel dining-room
and the captain from an unfortunate encounter on my first
arriving at the town and looking for a taxi. Neither of them
remembered me. They were informally dressed in sweaters
and corduroy trousers, and they were playing very well, standing back from the table and driving the celluloid ball with
great force. I couldn't help watching the game and switching
my head idiotically as I talked.

'You people have been so deuced long making that film.
We thought you'd finished.'

I explained as best I could that we'd hardly begun.

'It's an awful nuisance, you know. The men don't like it
at all. They say they get no time for writing home.'

'But wouldn't they,' I asked, 'be out on manœuvres, anyway?'

'Good heavens, no. We'd never drive them the way you
film people do. They wouldn't stand it.'

'I'm awfully sorry if it's a nuisance . . .'

'That's all right. I don't suppose it's your fault entirely. The
War Office have told us to co-operate so we'll have to do what
we can.'

'Do you mind, old boy? I think that ball went between your
legs.'

The major started to crawl under a bench. The captain lit
his pipe.

'Well. We'd better do what they want, Bob.'

'Just as you think, Charles.'

'A platoon and a sergeant,' I reminded them tentatively.
'And if you two gentlemen will come along too . . .'

The major looked up from the floor.

'I say. Can't you get us a few photographs of film stars?'

'Sexy ones,' said the captain, making vicious swipes at the air, 'for the mess.'

'Perhaps you could collect them when you come over,' I suggested, as I thought, craftily.

'Come and help me look for this damn' ball, Bob. That's an order.'

They both crawled off down the room.

'You want a sergeant do you? I suppose we shall have to take Druker.'

'Oh, do we have to?'

'Anyway, it'll mean no beastly parade this afternoon.'

'Cheers.'

The major stood up, dusting the knees of his trousers.

'I'll send you over to Sergeant Druker. He'll pick the platoon and go with you. Captain Verity and I will follow on later. Would you mind going out into the passage and calling "Orderly"?'

I did so. After a considerable interval a small man with wire glasses appeared smoking a cigar. This he laid carefully on a window-sill before presenting himself in the room.

'Wilkins. Take this gentleman over to Sergeant Druker, would you?'

'Why can't he wait until I'm dummy?' said Wilkins, not inaudibly.

'By the way, when you come back, Wilkins, you might help Captain Verity to find our ping-pong ball.'

'Oh bother,' said Wilkins. 'Here, I'll lend you mine, sir. Only don't lose it again.'

'Thanks awfully, Wilkins.' The captain climbed out from under the sofa. Wilkins handed the major a ball from his pocket.

'Thanks. If you like you can borrow the "Monopoly" this evening, Wilkins.'

'Well. Cheerio for now. We'll be along later,' said the major.

'Thank you, sir,' I answered doubtfully.

And as he led me out of the room I heard Wilkins mutter, 'Monopoly, child's game. Trust them to hang on to the Mah Jong.'

Whereas the men's hut had reminded me of the quarters given over to the hourly boys, and the ping-pong room some pleasant school play-room utterly different from anything connected with the Film Unit, I found Sergeant Druker's office strongly reminiscent of the cell-like hotel bedroom from which Doris carried on her organization. The same elaborate lists and schedules festooned the walls, the same typewriters, carbon papers and tins of cigarette-stubs littered the tables. The sergeant himself was a middle-aged, grizzled man whose head, like the head of a horse, seemed slightly thinner than his neck. His features were long and colourless and he had strong yellow teeth which he bared in a series of taut, business-like grimaces. In his presence the orderly, Wilkins, stiffened convulsively. The sergeant immediately grasped the situation.

'Yiss,' he said. 'Thought you'd want me. The message-must-have-gone-wrong. A platoon you say, Wilkins? Fall in four men at wance. Jardine wan, Elvers tew, Marell three. Yourself four.'

'Excuse me.'

'Yiss.'

'I'm officers' orderly . . .'

'Miss.' The sergeant sprang at the 'phone. 'Get me Major Lambert. I'm sorry, sir. Yes, sir. It's about Wilkins. They need him in this film, sir. I believe Sprott knows the fishmonger quite well, sir. All right, sir. No, I'm afraid I 'ave no ping-pong balls, sir. Yes, sir. Right, Wilkins. Fall them in outside at wance.'

'I knew they'd need someone who understood acting,' he

said to me when Wilkins had disappeared. 'Will I have to dew my "Frontier Outpost's Farewell" to-day?'

'I don't know,' I said.

'Just-when-you-please. I've always-got-it-by 'art.'

Out of the window I saw the four disgruntled men form into a row.

'Will we be late back?'

'I couldn't say . . .'

He looked at me contemptuously, contriving to make me feel extremely inefficient.

' 'Phone the wife. Miss. 5327. Lilian. What yew got? Can't eat it. Might be poison. Look here. Got this acting on. No. They don't know what time. Well. You'll 'ave to get me something, won't you? Unless-you-want-to-poison-me. See you to-night.'

'Let's go,' he said to me, almost softly as he led me out; but as soon as he saw his fellow-artists his voice rose again to a staccato bellow.

'Chins-back, stomachs-in, thumbs-behind-the-seams-of-the trousers. Wan-tew-three number . . .'

So we set off in military formation, the sergeant leading.

The sun strengthened and almost burnt the back of my neck; we followed the cliffs round, walking, it seemed, on the thin white rim to the vast cup of the sea. I felt suddenly happy and excited at the prospect of seeing and helping in the making of a film for the first time. I trailed my feet along the path, as I had in childhood, and sent up little clouds of white dust. I looked round at the men with me. Behind the sergeant's back they had broken step, were slouching along with their hands in their pockets and generally behaving in a most unmilitary fashion. Now and then the youngest, a big, handsome, fair-haired boy with blue eyes and great dangling hands, would run up close behind the sergeant and parody his stiff strut, causing the rather scholarly-looking Wilkins to clap his hand

to his mouth and double up with suppressed laughter. At first
I was embarrassed by their childishness and tried hard not to
notice; but they plucked at my sleeve and nudged me until
I consented to watch the antics of one of them, a sharp-faced
little man with very shiny black hair. This one went sidling
up behind Sergeant Druker, and with a theatrical flourish produced an Ace of Spades from between the shoulders of his
battle-dress. I was nervous of the sergeant turning round and
involving me in their pranks, and most relieved when we
reached the scene of the location.

As soon as we met the unit the sergeant greeted Doris like
an old friend, and they walked off studying lists and schedules
together. Again I was struck by their similarity and the obvious
pleasure they both had in points of organization. I told Bert
that the two officers had said that they would follow on
directly, and then I wandered over to where the soldiers were
now lying on the grass. I had some vague idea that they might
escape and that I ought to be keeping an eye on them.

They had taken off their battle-dress tops and rolled them
for pillows. The large, shapeless uniform trousers made even
the smallest of them, Wilkins, loom large and bulky. They lay
there immobile, with the sea and the sky behind them, and I
had the first, sharp feeling of their independence and isolation
from the rest of us. After a week spent confined with the
obsessions and intrigues of the Film Unit, it was an independence I envied.

'Eleven o'clock,' said the nearest as I approached. 'Pre-war
just time for a nice cup of chocolate with a drop of cream and
and a few nice Bath Olivers. You're new, aren't you?'

'Yes,' I said.

'You'll have a job with us, you know. Bleeding temperamental, we are. Aren't we, lad?'

'Nark it,' said the youngest, tired.

'That's Mr. Ellvers. Private bleeding temperamental Gary

Cooper by now,' said the first by way of introduction. 'Then there's Mr. Wilkins, all-round chess champion of the section. Very talented body of men we are. And Mr. Marvell, ex-conjuror or bleeding illusionist, known as Mr. Ruddy Marvell. And yours truly, Mr. Jardine. Now you know us all.'

'Yes,' I said.

I sat down beside them and they lay in silence for some time. Presently the boy, Ellvers, fell asleep.

Marvell produced a pack of cards and began to shuffle them in the most extraordinary way, multiplying and reducing them until at one moment he held only one card and at another he was juggling with about three packs. None of his companions paid the slightest attention to this feat.

'Do you think Major Lambert will be long?'

'Depends on how the balls last out,' said Wilkins, gazing out to sea.

'I suppose acting in a film is something new to most of you,' I said.

'Look here, boy,' said Jardine. 'We're in the army, see? We do what we're told, don't we? If we're told to sit about on our cans for a few months and get put on the pictures we do it. It's for the major to say, and if he says it's O.K. then it is. But if you think we wouldn't rather be sitting down to a nice slice of the old pork and apple-sauce like we had pre-war at home to being out on this lark, then you're wrong, see? Isn't that so, Wilk?'

'Definitely,' said Wilkins.

' 'Course I won't speak for the boy. The boy, he rather fancies himself as a film star.'

They all looked round affectionately at Ellvers. The wind was blowing his hair over his sleeping eyes. His bare forearms, crossed defensively, rose and fell on his chest.

'But then he has a bastard time on parades.'

'Sergeant's got it in for him.'

'So he's glad of the change, see?'

Sparks Henry, the cameraman, came past with a tripod. He set up the camera and looked through a sort of smoked monocle. Then he held out a little clock and made a reading. Then he walked round looking through a long, square instrument. Sparks had once kept a photographer's shop in a small Lancashire town. When he had photographic apparatus in his hand he was perfectly happy and confident, and his camera work was of a high order. But away from cameras he was stupid and malicious to an extraordinary degree. Most of the time he spent describing quite imaginary scenes in which he had told Very Important People in language of great obscenity exactly what he thought of them.

'Hullo, lads. Hullo you,' he said when he had finished his preparations. 'What's up?'

'We're waiting for the major,' I explained.

'Bloody snob. Who does he think he is?' Sparks exploded, 'Keeping us hanging about like this. Last time he did I told him straight. I said, "Who do you think you are?" I said. "General Montgomery?" I said. "You can take your bloody crowns off your shoulders," I said, "and you know what you can do with them." '

'Sparks,' said Marvell quietly. He had three cards before him in the grass. 'I wonder where she's gone.'

'And that little runt of a captain too. I told him straight I did . . . You wonder where who's gone?'

'The Queen. Look. She must be one of these three cards. But which one? Have a shilling on it?'

'All right. That one. "Little runt," I said . . . Ha-ha, I've won.'

'Yes. Have another go.'

' "We're making this film for the Government", ' I said. 'I've won again!'

'Yes. Why not have a bit more on this time? Have ten bob on.'

'Make it a quid.'

'All right.'

'Oh, I've lost.'

'Yes.'

'Damn! Make it another quid.'

'All right.'

'I've lost again.'

'Yes.'

'Damn you! You're a ruddy Marvell you are.'

He pushed back his pork-pie hat and walked away scratching his head. The other soldiers laughed gently.

Time passed. Dorcas and I brought up the tea. Ellvers slept. The sergeant conspired with Doris. Daisy battered away on her typewriter. Angela sat reading a detective story in her car. Crankshott, the sound man, wired up the microphone and then lay on the grass working out quadratic equations. Sparks told Bert how rude he had once been to a first assistant in the silent days. There was still no sign of the officers.

'Isn't there anything we can shoot without them?' I asked Doris, but she said they were in all the scenes scheduled for that day.

Marvell did incessant conjuring tricks. The hourly boys crept round him and gazed with stunned admiration. I was afraid he was going to take all their money off them at 'Spot the Lady', but he didn't suggest it. He seemed quite content to be entertaining them. At first, when I had gone into the soldiers' hut, I had been struck with the resemblance between them and the hourly boys. Now I saw the difference: they were cleverer, quieter, more adult. They were different from all of us.

Lunch time.

'Pre-war, a picnic basket on the cliffs would have been the order of the day,' said Jardine. 'Melton Mowbray pie. A few hard-boiled eggs. Thermos of coffee . . .'

And as he spoke the captain appeared on the cliff path, climbing towards us. When he arrived he stood with his hands in his pockets and looked round him in some amusement.

'Frightfully sorry, you people,' he said. 'But the major can't make it.'

'Why not?' asked Doris, stepping forward angrily.

'He had to go into town. Most important. Frightfully sorry and all that.'

And he turned away.

'Who's going to tell the director?' asked Doris. The four assistants hung their heads. Angela closed her detective story.

'I'll tell him,' she said, 'I'll drive back now.'

As the captain passed me he whispered. 'Frightfully sorry, old chap, but the major simply had to get into town before the shops closed. We just had to have some more ping-pong balls.'

And as he left the clouds darkened, the sea faded into the sky, and with the arrival of some depression from over the Atlantic, it once more settled in to rain.

VII

The Sergeant and the Miracle

NATURALLY THE whole tone of the unit, during the wet days that followed, was one of bitter hostility to the army. Sparks's imaginary interviews became more and more profane, Doris plotted letters to the War Office, even Crankshott, the sound man, usually so involved in problems of sound engineering that he hardly noticed what was going on around him, suggested sending in a bill to the captain for the sound-track wasted in recording his limericks.

This fierce resentment had the effect, as nothing else could have done, of binding the unit together. There was little talk of sacking, and even the scriptwriter was sympathized with by Doris for having his script so 'bitched about' by the stupidity of the soldiers. He, himself, was so disgusted by the major's callousness that he dwelt more and more on the chivalrous and efficient officers he had known in his youth, and from his talk of the script it seemed that it was them he was describing rather than the actual military specimens we had come down to study.

'Ping-pong!' he said when I told him the story. 'Fencing and polo were the only games recognized by the officers at Loamhurst.'

Tactfully I forbore to mention clock golf.

Angela had disappeared upstairs with the director. He, we were told, was making cast-iron plans for the film, and for our expedition overseas; at any rate he remained hidden. How his wife's affairs were going I couldn't find out. This was a

peaceful and straightforward period in the unit, and I don't
think I need describe it further. More important, from the
point of view of my story, was an evening I spent with the
soldiers at a dance in the town. I was in a position then, as
was no other member of the unit, to find out certain things
which threw considerable light on later events.

I may say that I didn't fully share our people's dislike of
the soldiers. They were polite enough to me, and when I met
one or two of them about the town they always seemed
pleased to see me and asked how I was getting on. The hotel
food not having improved a great deal of my time was spent
in tea-shops, and it was in one of these that I met Mr. Jardine,
lugubriously surveying the menu.

'Pre-war,' he started dolefully, and I made haste to interrupt
him.

'How are you?'

'Fine. Fine. Getting busier too. How are you? Working
hard?'

'Scarcely.'

'Never become a bleeding Frank Capra if you let the old
talent rust in idleness, will you?'

'I suppose not.'

'Still. Relaxation never did no one no harm.'

'No.'

'Lovely relaxations we had, pre-war. Fish teas. Drives into
the country. Strip off and into the old swimming pool. Real
relaxations they were.'

'Yes.'

'Don't get it now.'

'No.'

'Still, talking of relaxation we're giving a small hop at the
Naafi to-night. Care to come along? Sure the boys would like
to see you.'

'That's very kind of you. I'd like to very much.'

I felt extraordinarily pleased and flattered.

''Course, it won't be like the dances some of us can remember. Case of "Who's coming out for a cool in the carpark?" that was. Pre-war . . .'

There was a big Naafi in the centre of the town, and it was here that the dance was given by men from all the forces stationed round about. When I got there I soon recognized, grouped round the bar, the men from the section up on the cliffs. Wilkins, Marvell and Jardine crowded round me, and in the crush of dancers I saw Ellvers dancing with the small, pretty girl whom I had seen on my first night at the hotel dining with the major.

'Good evening,' said Wilkins. 'We're delighted to see you.'

'Nice to see you all again,' I said, tapping the wet bar for drinks.

'Well, there's one you won't see here to-night, praise the Lord,' Marvell ejaculated piously.

'Who's that?'

'Sergeant Druker. He's got a date somewhere else.'

'To everyone's relief,' said Wilkins.

'To yours anyway, Wilk.'

'Well, yes. I happened to be running over the *Observer* chess problem in my head during parade. Of course, when the sergeant said left-turn I automatically advanced two squares and muttered "Check." I'm not really allowed out to-night.' And Wilkins smiled slightly at his own daring.

They all looked extremely clean and shy, and each had his hair smoothed down with water.

'I'd rather not have him here for the cabaret,' said Marvell, 'And I bet Lilian feels the same.'

'Lilian?'

'Yes, Lilian Druker. His wife, you know. There she is dancing with the boy.'

'Oh, yes. I saw her one night at the hotel, having dinner with Major Lambert.'

'We're not,' said Jardine firmly, 'having a word said against our Lil. That right, boys?'

And Wilkins and Marvell agreed, in chorus.

I covered up my *gaffe* by collecting and distributing the glasses of beer. Each raised his politely to me, bowed slightly from the waist and then, after taking a sip, put his glass down on the counter.

'With all respect to you,' said Jardine. 'Pre-war we should have told them to put *that* back in the horse.'

'Pity we couldn't shoot anything the other day.' I hastily changed the subject.

'Well there, you know that Captain Verity, him and Major Lambert, they don't take your filming seriously.' Jardine became consoling. 'Of course I'm too old to care much for myself, but I think it'll be a nice thing for, say the boy there, to have himself in a picture.'

'Nice for all of us,' said Marvell.

'That's what I say. Of course, the boy, he's most delighted about it. Goes to the cinema and sees just how big his name'll be on the front part. Silly really,' Jardine giggled, 'but you can see his point.'

This seemed a change from their attitude on the cliffs, and I wondered if the idea of the film was getting a hold on them, whether they would come to take an interest in it and co-operate with the unit. Although this never happened, or had a chance to happen, I did notice later in them, and particularly in Ellvers, a sort of bashful yearning to be on the screen, if it could be done without too much loss of independence.

'A man doesn't get much credit on a job like ours,' said Wilkins. 'Perhaps your film will make people realize . . . Funny the officers are so against it.'

'They don't understand; it needs a film to give a true picture of what we do.' There was something slightly priggish in this remark of Marvell's, and my answer, now I remember it, seems equally so.

'I hope ours will be true. I know the director will try and make it true. That's why he's anxious not to use actors, but men like you who've had no experience of playing a part.'

'Well, I wouldn't say that . . .' Jardine held up his hand. 'Sergeant, he's done his monologues.'

'Old hat,' said Marvell.

'Old hat they may be, Ruddy, still it's playing a part. Funny the boy's never done any performing—wouldn't even sell programmes at the camp concert; but he takes to this job like a duck to water. 'Course Ruddy's had experience in the illusion line. That's why he's in this do to-night.'

'What's on the programme to-night?'

'Quite good. An A.T. contortionist. An R.A.F. imitates railway trains. Then I do "The Miracle of the Disappearing Lady".'

'Who disappears?'

'Why, Lil of course. She's perfect for it. Small and pretty, and can tuck herself away in a second. Of course, the cabinet is just one I rigged up in camp. I couldn't get any steel, not for Severing the Lady once she's helpless inside.'

'How would the sergeant like your vanishing his wife?'

'He'd be mad. I daren't suggest it to her until I knew he wouldn't be here. She's a real sport, though, she agreed in a minute.'

Then Ellvers and Mrs. Druker came up; I bought them beers and was introduced.

Mrs. Druker smiled at me and pointed to Ellvers.

'When are you going to take some more photos of him?' she asked.

'When it stops raining.'

'Oh, do take some more soon.'

Her admiration for him was obvious, and Ellvers smiled and
looked furtively proud. The music started again, and putting
one of his big hands gently on her waist, he steered her back
on to the floor.

After the interval came the cabaret and, while the A.T.
stood in the spotlight and peered tentatively out from between
her legs, I had another conversation with Mrs. Druker.

'Aren't you nervous of vanishing?' I asked.

'Sometimes I think it'd be the best thing for me.'

I was so surprised I looked round full at her.

'What?'

'To vanish.'

But before she could explain Marvell came bustling up.

'Better go and get changed now, Lil,' he said.

'So long, Lil,' said Ellvers. 'Be sure and come back.'

'If I don't, Ruddy, just vanish him too.'

'He wouldn't like that. I might send him where there
weren't any pictures,' Marvell laughed.

I felt an impending mystery and would almost have encouraged Jardine to talk about pre-war food. The big room,
crowded with men in uniform, was dark and smoky and suddenly quite silent. In the white dust of the spotlight the A.T.
was subsiding tremulously and unnaturally in the splits. Only
an occasional cough or the scrape of a boot on the polished
floor broke the tense and admiring stillness. As I drank my
beer I heard Wilkins mutter beside me.

'Cryptic, did you think?'

'What?'

'That talk of vanishing.'

'Slightly.' The A.T.'s limbs assumed a more natural arrange-
ment. A barrage of claps and whistles and then, once more,
silence as the R.A.F. capered into the limelight, his hands
cupped about his mouth. From him came puffs and squeaks
and whistles, marvellously train-like, and, to the background

of this remote and faintly sinister human railway, Wilkins
went on whispering, with more emphasis than I had ever
heard from him before.

'But it would be the best thing for her. That man's a swine.
You know the music-hall sergeant-major. This one isn't a
joke. It's not only us. We suffer from him, of course; that's
part of our job. But it's her we're sorry for. We all know
the life he's giving her. Even the major knows about it.
That's why he took her out, to see if he could help her.
We'd all do anything for her. Who wouldn't? Here she is,
look.'

The R.A.F. had disappeared with a final shriek. Two soldiers
carried in the cabinet, hung with black-out material, and
turned it round and round before the audience. Marvell came
in and banged its sides ostentatiously. Then Lil walked into
the cold pool of light and stood before the dark, almost
coffin-like box, shivering slightly.

Dressed only in a spangled brassiere and trunks she looked
naked, very young, frightened and chilly. I felt in my companions, and in the whole audience, a surge of sympathy.
There was an anxiety that the trick would go off well for her
sake, that she should be vanished neatly, neatly re-materialized
and not be away too long or feel any discomfort in the
process. Marvell seemed to feel this also, because he helped
her into the cabinet in a most gentle and courteous way,
pattering in a soothing fashion the whole time.

Marvell's hand was on her bare arm. She was standing in the
cabinet, her bright flesh and ornaments sharply divided from
the black background as if she was a little flat puppet cut out
of paper. The music had stopped and there was a tremulous
silence. Again there was a feeling that this was really rather
an alarming experience for her, a hope that she wasn't minding
it and a relief when she was seen to be smiling. And then the
silence was filled with a great bellow.

'Good. A cabaret. I will now recite "The Frontier Out-post's Farewell". What, you? You filthy little tart!'

And then things happened more quickly than I can des-cribe. Sergeant Druker, leaving another woman's side, was seen to crash out of the darkness into the limelight. Ruddy Marvell jumped into the cabinet beside Lil and drew the curtain. The sergeant swore and pulled the curtain back. There was a roar of laughter as he beat about in the emptiness. Then Jardine said 'Run for it.' I was caught up with the rest as they fought through the crowd for an exit door. We all fell out into the street as Ruddy emerged with his greatcoat draped round Lil. Ellvers ran up to her and wrapped her round with a desperate embrace.

'I'm not,' she said, only a little breathlessly, 'a bit frightened.'

'Come with us,' said Jardine.

'No,' she said. 'I'm going home. I'm not frightened.' She kissed Ellvers and seemed to faint for an instant; but she revived, and handing Ruddy his coat, walked firmly back into the hall for her clothes.

'He better wait till we get over on the other side, that's all,' said Ruddy.

'I know you'll forgive us; but I think it would be better if we got back to camp,' said Wilkins.

'A man like that would have had his face bashed in,' said Jardine, 'pre-war.'

And they left me.

There was only one detail that I didn't remember until afterwards. The woman with Sergeant Druker was Doris.

VIII

The Accident

I HAVE NO doubt that after this incident things went badly for the soldiers, and I believe they became more than ever difficult to organize. During the following days I stayed at the hotel doing some of Doris's work, among it the incredibly complex computation of the wages due to the hourly boys, while she went out to the cliffs where they had now begun actually filming. The day came, however, when I had finished the accounts and I also went out on location, saw, for the first time, the director, saw some film being shot, and was present at that extraordinary, ghastly occurrence which was the chief incident of my film career, and forms, as it were, the pivot of my story.

This happening was so strange and significant, and so altered my view of the people involved, that I find it difficult to remember in detail the events which led up to it. Everything that went before is overshadowed in my mind, just as everything that followed after is dramatically overlit. I should like to state it as shortly as possible, and yet I feel that I must make an effort to recall the exact situation if its precise and peculiar nature, about which there were afterwards so many opinions, is to be properly explained.

That morning we were shooting some cliff-scaling exercises. Sergeant Druker and the same platoon, Wilkins, Ellvers, Marvell and Jardine, were on the cliffs, hauling each other up from ledge to ledge with climbing ropes. The particular incident in the story being filmed was explained to me later on by the scriptwriter, and I will let him tell the story, when the time comes, in his own words. For the moment I will recall how I arrived on the cliff-top and met the unit, and was told by Doris to go along the cliffs and fetch the director, who had strolled off down a path to think things over until they should be ready to shoot.

I walked off down the track I had known from childhood. My view was constantly obstructed by some buttress of chalk, and I did not know round what sudden corner I should come upon the director. Once again I was excited. Now, after all this preparation, I was really to meet this superman and see him at work. I hoped that, to-day, nothing would go wrong, that the soldiers would be amenable. The sun was shining. Above me the cameras, microphones and reflectors were waiting to record—what? Life? Adventure? Art? I didn't know, but I felt it to be something immensely important and impressive. And the man who was to do it all, whom I was to help do it all, was somewhere in front of me, standing gazing, as I imagined, at the sea, seeking, I had no doubt, some of its vast compelling power, some of its unutterable poetry.

When I did see him it was as one of a group standing at the end of an upward path, several yards above me. He stood with his back to the sun so that his features were indistinguishable; one gesticulating hand held a script, the other a shooting-stick. Before him, at a lower level, stood two other figures, his wife and the scriptwriter. As he spoke I stood still and none of them noticed me.

'Who typed this script?'

'I did it last night,' Angela almost whispered.

'I should have guessed by the mistakes. How do you think you spell sergeant?'

'S . . .'

'Oh, imbecile. Anyway, I can work without it. Why does no one tell me when they're ready?'

I opened my mouth; but he had already turned away and was climbing hurriedly to the cliff-top. As he went his hand fluttered towards the sea and sent the white paper sailing down through the air. In a moment he was out of sight, then returning on the grass verge above our heads.

Far more slowly Angela and the scriptwriter turned in the opposite direction. He put his hand on her waist; but she, seeing me at once, shook off his embrace. We all walked back silently along the lower level.

'Stay down there,' shouted Bert through his megaphone when we got under the unit. 'We may need you to give signals.'

'We'll stay with you,' said Angela.

We all three crouched in a little cave, such a cave as I'd hid in a hundred times on holidays, and from here we watched the shooting.

We were perched in the side of one buttress. Opposite us was a similar buttress, and the sea ran up an inlet between. About ten yards from the cliff-top opposite was a ledge, and on this ledge the action of the scene was taking place. So the camera was an eye staring down, and the microphone a long finger dangling towards this natural stage set against the back-cloth of water. The inlet was very narrow, so we in our cave were nearer, I suppose, to the performers than the unit on the top; although what signals I was supposed to give them I had no idea. All the instructions were given from above in a clipped, military fashion by the director.

Angela spread her fur coat and sat down to light a cigarette. A seagull glided listlessly past us.

'What's supposed to be happening?' I asked the script-writer.

As he told me the story of the scene he sat down and I squatted by him to listen. I don't think I was watching the action on the ledge very closely, although I have the feeling that it was going on all the time, and that it bore out, more or less, what he was saying.

'The whole film,' he started, 'shows the adaptation of this group of men to army life. At first the sergeant stands for all they hate most, discipline, brutality, ruthless efficiency. In the preliminary sequences, those we are shooting during their training in this country, we show the steps by which they come to like and respect him.'

I smiled to myself and stared down to the beach. I could see the objects on it quite clearly, stones, seaweed, driftwood floating on the foamy margin of the sea, where the water looked like dirty ginger-beer froth left in the bottom of a glass.

'The youngest, Ellvers,' he went on, 'is the most unhappy at first. He hates the training and particularly loathes the sergeant, who he feels always picks him out for fatigues and so on. . . .'

I looked back at the scriptwriter, by now quite interested in his story, and forgetting how differently it might have been told.

'But in this sequence something happens which starts a friendship between them. They have to help each other . . .'

I looked across to the ledge, and, as I say, as far as I can remember, the action on it followed his description.

'During the cliff-scaling Ellvers and the sergeant are left as the two last to be hauled up from a certain ledge. Ellvers looses his nerve and, when the rope comes down he can't move to tie it round him. He expects some volley of parade-ground abuse, but instead the sergeant ties him in, tells him it'll be all right, that he was just as scared himself at first but that there's nothing to it. Ellvers lets himself be pulled up and then helps the others pull up Druker. It's the beginning of a new feeling about danger for him, and a new comradeship with the sergeant. . . . They'll do the long shots first. They shouldn't be long over those. They won't need more than two of them. . . .'

'Cut!' The director's voice came faintly from above. 'All right. Print that one.'

'He's got one in the bag already,' said Angela. 'He's doing well this morning.'

'The main theme of our story, you see, is . . .' Angela brought out sandwiches. From above there were shouts of 'Reloading!' . . . 'Tea, Dorcas' . . . 'The gradual acquisition, by ordinary nervous individuals . . .' The scriptwriter went on. The seagulls swooped again, rose with the green of the sea reflected on their bellies, called, and turned inland. . . . 'In preparation for one single operation . . .' I felt the sun on my face. It was getting hotter . . . 'of courage. A quality that so few people understand. I hope the director will be able to get it across. I was brought up, you know, among men of great courage; but they never referred to it. I doubt if they understood it either. Perhaps it's something you mustn't understand, like love. A basic virtue. . . .'

'Stand by . . . O.K., roll them. *Action.*'

The camera started again. The scriptwriter's voice sunk to a whisper, which was lost in the shuffle of the sea.

'. . . St. Paul had a military nature, he should have known . . . Faith, Hope and Charity . . .'

Angela twisted round to watch the action. I looked round with her. Sergeant Druker was alone on the ledge, reaching for the rope which squirmed above his hand like a serpent.

'. . . The force behind all these is courage.'

The large brown figure was hoisted and swung off the chalky platform. Then something cracked in the air, and, it seemed a long time after, there was a thud and a splash on the narrow margin of the sea. I don't remember a cry.

In the time that passed later, when I alone of the unit was left standing on the cliff-top, a gradual revulsion of feeling came over me. This frightful accident, I thought, is in some way our responsibility; if we hadn't been there playing at film-making it might not have happened. So I was determined to wait for the major, however long he might be coming, and by my presence in some way to make amends. Although they hadn't liked him I felt that the sergeant had been one of the soldiers, and by allowing anything to happen to him we had, in some way, horribly outraged them.

So I felt as I stood and watched their figures on the beach. The sun threw their thin shadows back over the naked sand. I noticed a leisureliness, even a carelessness in their movements as one of them, faced with lifting the canvas-covered burden, took off his jacket for the work and then, perhaps feeling the small, sharp wind that had blown up, thought better and put it on again. At last they started off in procession. Did the unit realize the dreadful significance of this afternoon? Probably not; they were so obsessed with their own concerns, shut up in the unreal world of their work. But I was sure the soldiers realized; sure, as I watched their tiny, bowed and solemn figures, that they realized how tragic and ominous was the death of one of their leaders. Half-consciously I tried to join in their griefs and forebodings; but separated from them as I was by the sheer distance of the cliffs I felt like a stranger who watches a funeral from the gallery of a great cathedral, and wishes he could mourn and pay tribute, with the little knot of relatives, to the sacred memory of the dead.

At last I saw the major and captain arrive on the beach, and one of the soldiers must have pointed me out to them, for they started up the paths that led to where I was standing.

Perhaps, as I went on thinking things over, I had forgotten the curious scene in the Naafi and was quite persuaded by the scriptwriter's description of the sergeant, the austere, competent, but finally warm-hearted leader. At any rate, I thought of the danger to Major Lambert and the whole expedition in the loss of such a man. I wanted to say something of that sort to him when he came up the path; but when he got up to me I couldn't speak at all.

'You better get back home,' he said. 'Try and forget what you saw.'

'If there was any negligence on our part . . .'

But the major only said, decisively. 'He shall have military honours.'

'Yes, of course, sir.' I went on, 'I can't imagine how it happened. None of us thought there was any danger.'

He looked at me as if I was mad. Either he knew exactly how it had happened or thought it quite unimportant.

'If there's anything any of us can do . . .'

'I shall let you know.'

'Thank you, sir.'

He looked at me encouragingly and offered his cigarette case. The captain asked the question that had been in my mind all the afternoon.

'After this, are you still going on with the bloody film?'

The major saved me from answering.

'Oh, we shall have to send a report into the War Office. I expect they'll tell us what to do.'

'Anyway, we shall all try and keep it as quiet as possible.'

'Why?'

'I didn't think you'd want the story in the papers.'

'It isn't that I'd mind, it's . . . Well, the men have got a pretty tough time coming to them, anyway.'

As I stood puzzled he patted my shoulder.

'Don't you worry, old boy. Life's too short.'

They had both become almost cheerful again. They walked away towards the camp and ended our inconclusive interview.

IX

After the Accident: The Director

'WHAT A TERRIBLE thing for you, my dear. And so early in the run . . .' Mrs. Cooper talked, laying the cards patiently and circumspectly, awed, perhaps, by the solemnity of the subject, into playing with scrupulous honesty. I sat by her table in the lounge.

'I answered your mother's letter this morning. I spared her this news. I knew it would only distress her. I told her you seemed to be getting on well and enjoying the work; although I've seen so little of you lately.'

And yet we had all been in the hotel for the last three days. No one seemed to know if we were to start filming again, or if anyone in the unit had been in touch with the army authorities about the accident. The tragedy had confounded all our plans. An occurrence not allowed for in the schedules, there was some feeling that it would cancel the whole film and lead to our recall to London.

'By the way, your mother was asking if you had seen your director yet. She asked, if I remember, in the postscript. That's why I forgot to mention it sooner.'

'I've seen him at work; I haven't had a chance to speak to him so far.'

'Really?'

'He works very hard. He isn't about the hotel much,' I explained hurriedly.

'No, he does seem to keep a good deal to his room. I suppose he's very busy. And then the shock of this business on top of it all—it must have unnerved him.'

'None of us has been quite the same.'

'I know, dear. I always think a sudden death of that nature, on the stage, seems twice as terrible. We don't like to think of people caught out in disguise, as it were. Supers, you know, have had weights fall on them. And then poor Sir Henry, dying in his wig at Bradford; the account of it grieved me very much at the time, and I can assure you, it troubles my dreams to this day.'

The conversation was making me uncomfortable. Mrs. Cooper disturbed me, for although her voice was chastened and sympathetic, she was, I thought, smiling to herself as she put up a black nine.

'If you'll excuse me . . .'

'Of course. I expect you're busy too. The show must go on, mustn't it?'

'I want to find out.'

I decided to go up and see Doris. I still had a strong feeling of guilt about the whole affair and I wanted to make sure that the unit were making all amends possible to the major and the army authorities. Oddly I was not now at all nervous of my superiors, so clearly did I see myself as the only one, with the possible exception of the scriptwriter, who would know what to do in the circumstances. Accordingly it was with complete self-confidence that I knocked on Doris's door.

'Well?' she said, as I came in.

She was lying on her bed reading a best-seller the size of a telephone directory. It was the first time I had seen her in any way relaxed. I noticed that the schedules on her walls had not been altered, and that she had been washing her stockings in her hand-basin.

'I wanted to find out what's going to happen.'

'Your guess is as good as mine.'

'Are we going on with the film?'

'We'd have to start shooting all over again. And then I don't know who'll keep those men under control now he's gone.'

I looked at her, reflecting that she must have known the sergeant a great deal better than most of us. I remembered the night I had seen them out together.

'He'll be a great loss to the efficiency of the film.'

'And to that of the army, presumably.'

'Oh, yes. That too.' Against the clean, white pillow her face looked crumpled, a little soiled, a little frightened, as if part of her own power and authority had been balanced on the dizzy uncertainty of the cliff-tops.

'So there's no news.'

'No.' She covered her face with the novel. 'Oh, there's a letter for you on the table. It came addressed care of the unit.'

'For me?'

I crossed to the window and picked up a brown, typewritten envelope. For a moment I studied my own name.

'Well, what's the matter? Can't you read?'

'Oh. Do you mind?'

'What if I do? Read it for Christ's sake. Don't keep asking me what I'd mind.'

I read the letter. It was typed except for my name which had been written in at the top, and the major's signature. It asked the whole unit to the funeral, and said that we might go on filming afterwards. I am ashamed to say my first reaction was one of pleasure that it had been addressed to me. Then I showed it to Doris.

'Why should he want us there?' she asked.

I should like to have felt the obvious propriety of his invitation; but I didn't. However, I was ready to accept any proposal of the major's.

'I don't know. He says we may go on shooting afterwards.'

'So I see.'

'We'd better tell the director.'

'You go and tell him,' said Doris, seeming to disclaim all responsibility.

'All right,' I said, excited. 'Where is he?'

'In the snob's bar at the back of the hotel,' she replied with weary certainty, and I wondered if she had an accurate list of his hiding places for all hours of the day.

'I should think we'll have to work pretty hard on the film now,' I said; 'the major seems to want it made whatever happens.'

'Go down and see the director,' said Doris. 'And let me finish my book.'

'Here,' she added, stopping me on my way to the door, 'here's your letter.'

'Don't you want it for your file?'

'No, you keep it. It's written to you.' But whether she spoke kindly or bitterly I couldn't tell.

To the second floor I had the lift to myself. The lift man was horribly communicative.

'Ghastly tragedy. Saw it in the paper.'

'Yes.'

'Still, on with the motley, eh?'

How like Mrs. Cooper he was. I stared away into a mirror, but his face was there, grinning over my shoulder.

'The show comes first, I suppose, to you on the pictures.'

At the second floor the scriptwriter got in. He looked at me lugubriously.

'Hullo. Where've you been?'

'Up to see Doris.'

He seemed suspicious and said angrily. 'I suppose she's extremely annoyed at having her schedules put out.'

'Not altogether,' I answered. To-day I liked him less than usual.

'Of course it would be quite improper for us to start shooting again.'

'The major says we may.'

He lifted his eyebrows. Then, as we were still creeping towards the ground floor I asked, to change the subject, where the snobs' bar in the hotel was. I had never been there.

'At the back. You have to go through the dining-room,' and he added, with more animation, as we emerged into the hall, 'Are you going to get tight?'

'No. I have to see the director.'

'Oh, well, I'll be off then. Time to get in a couple of rounds of clock golf before the light fails.'

Going through the empty dining-room I thought only of my message. I felt none of the interest I should have had a week before at the prospect of talking to the director. Rather I felt a sort of hostility towards him and a contempt for the way in which he had hidden himself and left all the work to us. Yet when I pushed open the swing-door I couldn't help feeling a little of my former awe return. He was sitting so massively at the little table facing the entrance, so dominating the room in which everyone else looked shadowy and thin, so altogether oblivious of his surroundings and wrapped in some remote, personal abstraction while gazing into half a tumblerful of soda water.

The bar was the most recent addition to the hotel; it must have been built since the days when I used to stay there. Mirrors lined the walls and the lighting was of a honey colour which made one's reflection unusually handsome; but it could not disguise the fact that the director was pale, and it seemed to me, unshaven. As Angela had said, it was impossible to guess his age. His temples were grey, but that often comes early with his type of pure black hair. His face was deeply lined, but with furrows so characteristic that I can't imagine him ever having been without them. He was good-looking, but in the self-conscious way of an actor, so that the strength in his face seemed somehow over-dramatized. As I stood in front of him and he looked slowly up at me, coming, rather too obviously, out of his reverie, I suddenly had the peculiar and unnerving sensation of having seen him a great many times before, of having known him very well, but long, long ago in the past, in my earliest childhood. I gave him the letter and drew up a little chromium-plated chair beside him. He spoke at once, talking as if we had known each other and worked together in the greatest intimacy for years.

'This invitation,' he said; 'I don't understand it. It seems so theatrical.'

'On the cliffs it was the first thing he mentioned.'

'It will be interesting. I've never seen one. I remember we had a burial at sea once coming over from the States.'

He shocked me. I wanted to protest, but kept silence.

'A cook died of alcoholic poisoning.'

'Shall I answer it?' I asked sharply.

'Yes. Say we—we'll all be there.'

He sipped his soda water. And then he turned to me, and looking straight into my eyes, asked unexpectedly:

'How's your mother keeping?'

His own eyes were of a most chilling blue, expressing a strength emphasized by the puckering round them that could have been caused equally by humour or exhaustion. I answered automatically.

'She's very well, I think.'

'She wrote to me about you, you know. I haven't had time to reply. I believe we were at an art school together. I believe I remember her. She was a very serious girl, doing sculpture. I was trying to be a painter. Yes, I remember her quite clearly. Well, how are you enjoying life in the unit?'

'Very much up till now.'

'I'm sure you're not. There's only one person for whom life becomes bearable in a Film Unit, and that's the director.'

I don't think he was joking.

'Of course,' I said. 'I suppose we all want to be directors in the end.'

'Of course.'

The barman came up to us. The director ordered more soda water. I asked for a beer, for which he didn't volunteer to pay.

'When I gave up painting, for the cinema,' he went on, 'I know some people thought I was taking an easy way out. What nonsense! A painter is alone with his tubes and brushes —objects with no wills of their own. How easy for him to force them into his power. In the cinema we have human beings, life itself to contend with. A director must be an artist, a politician, and something of a dictator. What is the use of dreaming a film in your head unless you can put it into action? And to do that you must be able to control absolutely the thoughts and emotions, not only of your actors, but of the people who work for you. And then there is the money involved . . .'

At first I was interested in what he was saying; but, as I shouldn't have done a week before, I looked behind it for a motive. And I got the feeling, as I so often did when he spoke to me later, that he was desperately trying to convert me to something, to get me on his side.

'Doris tells me you're shaping very well,' he went on encouragingly. 'I'm sure you won't be impatient of the almost military discipline.'

I smiled.

'Ours is an exacting job. We must be as much on the lookout as the soldiers themselves; ever on the lookout for the stir in the bushes, the glow of a cigarette, the thin pillar of smoke which gives away the position of what we have to pin down and record—the exact truth. You don't think I exaggerate our importance?'

'Oh, no.' And I wondered why he bothered to say 'our'.

'I think it lies in our attachment to the present. I sit in here, for instance, because it is the most up-to-date part of the hotel. Working in the cinema the last twenty years is our period, there are no great ghosts, no immense Italians or shadowy Spanish to overawe us. Our medium abolishes the past. The present is our location. Chromium, glass and electricity. That's our setting. In front of it we reawaken the old legends, love and excitement and boredom, meeting and parting and now —war . . .'

He went on in this way for some time, now lashing himself into an angry argument, now throwing back his head and laughing at a joke of his own. Occasionally he would look round at me nervously to make sure I was still listening. I gave a polite murmur, but my attention had strayed. I had read his articles.

After a while he finished discussing general principles and started to talk about himself. I listened again and was fascinated by his detailed vanity.

'A director must keep in as strict training as an explorer or an officer. Now, when I'm preparing a film I work like this. I don't think of it until six o'clock. Then I come in here. I drink some soda water before I go upstairs to work. I change into old clothes and then walk up and down the room dictating to my wife. As I walk I find it helps me to flourish a shooting-stick. During dictation I smoke the fifty cigarettes my wife has rolled for me during the afternoon. This goes on until nine o'clock, when we eat. Fish, cereals, and more soda water. After that my wife goes out or to bed, and I sit up to work over details until three o'clock. Then I have a bath and sleep. In the morning I wake at ten and go to the gymnasium. Boxing and singlesticks . . .'

'Is there anything you'd like me to do for you now?' I asked suddenly, preventing him from telling me what he had for breakfast.

He looked at me suspiciously, hurt. I felt sorry and would have liked to have encouraged him with, 'And then, tea or coffee . . .' But it was too late.

'Yes.' He used a different, commanding tone. 'Yes. You can go and find my wife. It's time I started work.'

As I left he hardly nodded, and I was glad of the excuse to get away. I think our conversation was embarrassing because there was no sort of intimacy between us. I had been a distant audience, and yet I had had the feeling that the director was trying to establish an intimacy, as unsuccessfully as a matinée idol who, while giving a performance, is trying to make a personal friend of someone in the first row of the stalls.

I had Angela paged but she wasn't in the hotel. I walked straight out into the street with a vague idea of looking for her. I was glad, I remember, to get out of doors. I had a lot to think over. Two things were worrying me; two quite unconnected feelings which were yet similarly inexplicable. One was the accident on the ledge. I had never seen a fatal accident before, but I felt there was something peculiar about this one. Of course, I hadn't been watching all the time, but there seemed a sort of neatness and swiftness about it, almost as if it had been planned as part of the film. The other was my vague uneasiness at remembering the director's face. Perhaps I had seen him on the screen somewhere. I couldn't remember.

Six o'clock. The queues were shuffling into the cinemas and the trams were clanging up from the promenade. I passed the town hall and the drinking fountain just as they were turning the old men out of the public library. In the half-light the pin-points of colour from the traffic lights shone brighter. The tea shops were shutting and the bars were opening; the dark sea was disappearing into the blackness of the evening;

soldiers with shining hair and great polished boots were standing whistling at the street corners; I was out on a pointless search for a woman who might be in any of these bars, cinemas, tea shops or tall, white houses, and I felt, for the first time since I had left home, a sudden loneliness. I should have liked to have walked into one of the front doors and found my mother dispensing tea. She would have asked me all about my job, and I realized there was a lot I shouldn't have told her.

In the High Street I met Dorcas, Fennimore and Harold.

'Trying to find a pub the unit don't know,' Fennimore said. 'Can't afford big rounds.'

'That bastard Hepplethwaite follows us everywhere.'

'Bet he earns twice as much as we do.'

They made off suddenly, afraid, I suppose, of my joining them.

On the next corner I heard a friendly whistle. Jardine and Marvell were engaged in leaning against a shop doorway.

'How are you, cock?'

'All right, I suppose.'

'Nasty business, that.'

'Very nasty.'

'Sergeant, you may have gathered, wasn't our best chum. Still we shall feel the loss, eh Ruddy?'

'Certainly. Damn' good soldier.'

'So I believe.'

'One of the best. Efficient? Couldn't beat him for it.'

'Good soldier all right.'

'Personal matters aside, he was a bloody good N.C.O.'

' 'Course, he wasn't our best chum.'

'But as old Wilk would say . . .'

'De mortuis . . .'

'Would he?' I asked.

'Certainly. And mean it. Cultivated sort of ponce, Wilk.'

'And he'd be right. We shall feel the loss in the company.'

'And Lil unprovided.'

'We shall all feel the loss.'

They ended piously and Jardine offered Woodbines.

'Didn't make much of a splash in the papers,' he went on more conversationally. 'Pre-war that'd 've been headlines in the *Flag Unfurled*.'

'In the what?'

'*News of the World*. Now it's a little para among the scoutmasters.'

'Too much news,' said Marvell. 'That's what's wrong nowadays, too much bleeding news.'

'Happy, as Wilk would say, is the age that has no history.'
'I believe you.'

'Pre-war, now, I've bought a sixteen-page newspaper and no bloody news at all. Those were the days.'

' 'Course, there isn't to be an inquest.'

'Isn't there?' I hadn't thought about an inquest.

'No. Major called us all together and told us he'd fixed for there to be no inquest. We were just to go on with our work and forget about the whole thing.'

'Except for the funeral. There's to be a funeral.'

'Yes,' I said. 'We're all going.'

'Military funeral. Still, it's hard to forget the loss of a good N.C.O. like that.'

'Bad blow for the company. Only one way to forget a bad blow like that.'

'How's that?'

'Alcohol.'

'And for alcohol——'

'Must have the bees and honey.'

'The what?'

'Money. Small loan possible?'

Luckily my mother's last letter had contained a postal-order and Jardine knew a barmaid who would cash it.

I walked on, although there seemed very little chance of now finding Angela. The director's scheme of work would have to be altered for once. I turned down between a row of houses, some of which were bombed, and others, peeling and damp, seemed to cower into the shadows to hide a general air of dilapidation. A few belated children were out playing, and a troop of seagulls were fighting the sparrows for some mess in the middle of the road. I was just turning back when I recognized a long, black car and saw Angela getting into it.

'Hullo,' I said.

'Hullo. What's happened to the unit?'

'Doris is reading a novel . . .'

'Jesus!'

'The scriptwriter's out putting, your husband's drinking soda water and I've been sent out to find you.'

'Poor sweet,' she said, not specifying which of us she meant. And then, 'How did you know where to find me?'

'I didn't. I was just wandering about.'

'I went to see that sergeant's wife. The major gave me her address.'

'I say. How awfully nice of you.'

'Don't be silly. There was nothing I could say. She seemed quite bewildered.'

'Still, I don't think anyone else in the unit thought of going.'

'That boy was there. What was his name? Ellvers. I left him sitting with her. Really, he was being rather sweet.'

My admiration for Angela increased, although her driving hadn't improved. However, we got back. In the lounge she said:

'You're going to the funeral?'

'We were all asked to.'

'I suppose we shall have to go. I doubt if she'll want us there. She said she wanted as little fuss as possible. She's an awfully nice woman and quite sensible, only, naturally, a bit bewildered.'

'I'm sure she is.'

'And that boy was being so sympathetic. I felt almost in the way.'

'I'm sure you weren't.'

She went to find her husband. As they passed through the lounge on their way upstairs I heard him say:

'Fine. You're just in time. Now we can start work.'

Later on, on my way to bed, I heard the tapping of Angela's typewriter through the bedroom door, the director's footfalls and thump of his stick.

Two hours later and I am lying on my back. By my calculation Angela is in her bath and the director is sitting up drawing little diagrams of camera angles all over the script. Dorcas has been sick. Bert, who was once an airman, has taken his pills and lies waiting for the strong, artificial sleep to freeze him into forgetfulness. The scriptwriter is waiting, trembling, by the crack of his door. When Angela comes out of the bath he will whisper, and she will cross the passage to kiss him good night. Doris has reached the thousandth page. And now, in a swift, lucid moment between sleeping and waking, I see the director again.

I am ten and my mother and father are out to tea. I have come back from school and am alone in the house. I climb up the circular staircase into a cold spare bedroom, then up a ladder and push open a trap-door in the ceiling. I sneeze because of the dust in the loft. I crawl over the trunks and fenders, the bird-cage and the picture frames. Under a floorboard is my book and standing by a low, attic window, less lined than now but rough and rugged from the print of my mother's thumbs, greenish as is the colour of bronze, set on a pedestal, stands the director's head.

X

The Funeral and the Rushes

Sunday: we were all assembled in the windy churchyard. The sea swayed slightly between the granite tombstones. A chaplain sailed forward with the medals tinkling on his billowing surplice. The wind lifted the flag off the gun-carriage. The sergeant's wife stood alone in front of the square of soldiers, isolated like a commander.

If I had expected the major to use the occasion for some sort of pronouncement I was mistaken. He left the address to the captain, who stood by the wounded earth, clenched his fists, blushed and rattled out his words with forced severity. I have heard such a tone used by school prefects when their house has lost a match.

'. . . A pretty good type . . . I know he was looking forward to going out on the job . . . when the time came. Anyway, if you make a good show of it it will be due . . . to what he taught you . . . to a large extent . . .'

A handkerchief fluttered in Lil's hand. I looked at the director beside me. He was wearing a long, black overcoat, and his handsome face was suitably furrowed.

'. . . and our deepest sympathy . . . to Mrs. . . .'

Some of the high, curt words were blown away.

'All right. Company . . . Atten . . . shun.'

The empty gun-carriage was drawn off after the men.

Afterwards the major thanked us all for coming and refused our invitation to lunch in the hotel.

At lunch-time we were all subdued, and although no one

liked to talk of the funeral it seemed in some way irreverent
to speak of anything else. In the end Doris remembered that
the editor of the film was driving down that afternoon with
the rushes, that is to say, the developed negative of the film
we had already shot, and that we had arranged to see them
that afternoon in the local cinema. So our work made a
welcome distraction and we waited eagerly for the editor to
arrive. I think we had forgotten what we should see on the
rushes.

The editor was an extremely smart man in a camel-hair
coat and had smooth red hair, which he took every opportunity to comb. Although he had all the manners of a young
man he must have been over forty. His name was Alec, and
in the intervals of hair combing he kept swallowing little
white tablets from a silver box. He arrived in the lounge just
as we were having coffee—the first film editor I ever saw.

' 'Struth,' he said. 'Here you all are. What's the matter?
Look as you'd all been to a funeral.'

'As a matter of fact,' said the scriptwriter, 'we have.'

'And there's old William Shakespeare. Cheerful as ever. I
say, Doris. You've nearly had it, chum.'

'Oh,' said Doris, with carefully feigned indifference.

'Yes. Old Underling was binding like hell about the
amounts you've been letting the hourly boys charge in for
overtime. Says it's nearly five hundred pounds. Can't understand it when you've hardly been shooting anything.'

'Does that bastard see the accounts now?' asked Bert.

'He sees a bloody sight too much. So,' said Alec, 'to distract
his attention from things which didn't concern him I showed
him my new assistant.'

'What's she like?' said Angela.

'Smashing. Only seventeen. Big mouth, nice little figure,
wants to act. Of course I daren't let her touch the film. So to
save old Doris here, I had to sacrifice the poor kid to Under-

ling. The old swine has to go to tea with her aunt every Sunday in Isleworth.'

'Is she a good assistant?' said Daisy.

'Hopeless, my sweet. Only it does me a bit of good seeing her bend over the bins, and she's useful for Underling.'

'Best use for her,' said Daisy bitterly.

This studio gossip seemed to be cheering the unit up. A waiter passed.

'Got any gin?' said Alec.

'Yes, sir.'

'Bring me a bottle.' And he handed a five-pound note. We were soon all drinking very sticky gin and lime at Alec's expense.

'Oh, yes. Your name's mud up at the office. Schwartz thinks the public's tired of war films anyway, and wants to do a musical about the Women's Land Army.'

'Imbecile,' said the director.

'How is Schwartz?' Doris asked.

'Oh, he had a terrible time with his mother. She wanted to get into the unit, you know, but he bought her a tobacconist's shop in Wardour Street, and now she seems fairly happy; only she's got a Greek boy-friend who writes scripts and keeps bullying Schwartz about them. Schwartz is frightened of him.'

' Why?'

'He's an all-in wrestler. His scripts are about Federal Union or something.'

Alec gave half a tumblerful of gin to Dorcas who drank it and fell off his chair. Everyone laughed.

'Edifying, isn't it?' the scriptwriter whispered beside me.

When we'd finished the gin we drank whisky from Alec's flask.

'Well,' Alec asked, 'how's the picture?'

The director, still ice-cold sober, leaned forward in his chair to make a statement.

'We've had hold-ups, bad hold-ups, I admit. But, as you know, we shall soon be going over to the other side. I believe that with the story we have got already and the material we shall get over there we shall have something which will be . . .'

Dorcas groaned.

'Although one hesitates to use superlatives, naturally,' the director went on, ignoring the prostrate boy to whom Angela gave a glass of water, 'I can say we shall have the material for the greatest motion picture of our time. This operation is a superb opportunity for the unit, a superb opportunity.'

'Good,' said Alec. 'Well, I've got your rushes in the car.' He consulted a gold wrist-watch. 'I suppose we'd better get going.'

As we crowded into his car, a dove-grey Bentley even longer than Angela's, he said:

'Beats me this stuff. Did you use a dummy?'

No one answered, and we arrived at the cinema in rather inebriated silence.

It was two hours before the public would be allowed in and the commissionaire was still in his shirt-sleeves. We sat in the front rows, the director sprawling his legs over the back of the seat in front, Sparks, the camera man, squatting on the floor, and the continuity girl getting on with her knitting. Angela came and sat next to me.

'Have you got a note-book?' the director asked, 'there might be something.' And he closed his eyes.

'I've made a rough cut of this sequence,' said Alec, walking about with his coat still on. 'I didn't have anything else to do.'

'What does he mean?' I asked Angela furtively.

'Darling, you *are* ignorant. He means that he got the rushes in disjointed shots and he has joined them together in order to make a sequence.'

'Christ. Will we ever have anyone who knows anything about pictures?' Bert was behind us, I affected not to notice.

'Do you think his wife would like to see these?' Doris asked.

'Hardly,' said the scriptwriter coldly.

And we were plunged into darkness.

A number board appeared and disappeared on the screen. Then we saw Ellvers and the sergeant on the ledge.

'Action,' came the director's voice persuasively.

Ellvers looked up. On his face we saw a growing horror.

'Now look down, slowly, towards the sea.' The director's recorded words sounded like the instructions of a hypnotist.

He looked down fearfully. His whole body shrank in towards the rock. As it did so the sergeant fastened the rope round him.

'There was no close shot for this,' said Alec. 'I couldn't get the dialogue from the long shot, you were too far away.'

Ellvers looked up with the sergeant's hand on his shoulder. Slowly he was pulled up towards us. His eyes were closed and his lips worked. Then he reached the top.

'Now there's a close shot,' said the director.

Ellvers at the top: pushing back his cap and smiling, he unfastened the rope and lay down panting on the grass.

'Grand actor, you know, that boy.'

'So natural, too,' murmured Angela.

'Now,' said Alec. 'There ought to be a close shot of the sergeant fastening the rope round himself. But you've shot that from the cliff-top too.'

The next shot was the same as the first, only the sergeant was alone on the ledge. The rope dropped to a few inches above his head and he pulled it down. As he tied the knot he was smiling. Then he was in the air, his mouth and eyes opened and he fell. Again there was no sound of a cry. I felt Angela's arm against mine as she covered her eyes.

'That's what I don't get . . .'

'You bloody fool,' Doris screamed. 'Don't you realize that's what really happened? Don't you realize he killed himself?'

The lights went up and we all sat perfectly still.

Slowly the director uncoiled his legs. Then he said:

'Come back to the hotel, Alec. We must talk about the cutting of the first half of the picture.'

The rest of the unit followed them out, leaving Angela and myself alone in the stalls. I don't know why we waited, for there was nothing else to see.

'They ought to destroy that shot . . .' I began.

'Isn't it peculiar,' she said, 'that the rope should have pulled the boy up and then broken for the sergeant?'

I said nothing. I was still a little muzzy with Alec's gin, although I had avoided drinking too much of it. Her voice reached me echoing, from a long way off.

'I mean, the sergeant must have been a lot heavier.'

'I suppose so.'

'And there couldn't have been anything wrong with the rope because we saw it pull Ellvers up the moment before.'

I seemed to be seeing things clearly, but from a great height. There was something none of us had noticed before.

'Yes,' I said, 'But wait a minute . . . I mean no.'

'What are we talking about? Do you think there was something wrong with the rope?'

'No. But really it didn't pull Ellvers up just the moment before.'

'It did. We've just seen it on the screen.'

'Yes. But that was—— what did he call it, that editor?'

'A rough cut.'

'Yes. A rough cut.'

'What difference does that make?'

'Not much, really. Only that when you shot it there was some time between the two men being pulled up. Of course, when you see it on the screen you don't realize that. I seem to remember Dorcas getting the tea and all sorts of things happening in between . . .'

'So something might have gone wrong with the rope?'

'Yes.'

'What exactly?'

'I don't know.'

'I suppose to find out we should have to ask the people at the top of the cliff?'

'Yes. Do you think we should?'

'Perhaps we should leave it alone.'

'Perhaps we should.'

'It's too like a detective story,' Angela protested. 'You know, detective stories have always frightened me, not by their horrors but by their logic. Do you remember the Minotaur story where the prince starts out through the passages of the cave holding a skein of silk in his hand, knowing that he's going to meet a horrible monster at the end of it? I always feel like that when I start a detective story.'

'Do you feel like that now?'

'A bit.'

'Perhaps we'd better leave it alone, then.'

'Perhaps we had.'

'No. I tell you what. We'll go and ask his wife what she thinks about it. We'll ask her if she'd like to know any more details of the accident. After all, if there was anything wrong with the rope it was the unit's fault, and she'll get compensation or something. But if she doesn't want to make a fuss over it, then we needn't say any more.'

'How sensible you are, darling. Shall we go now?'

As we got outside, the queues were forming for the opening of the cinema, the commissionaire had got his braided coat on and the manager was standing in the foyer smoking a cigarette. He recognized Angela and asked her to sign a photograph for him. As she did so I felt very proud to be with her and almost forgot the tragedy in which we were involved.

'He must see a lot of awfully old films,' said Angela.

And then I reflected that she had got her mythology wrong. Theseus' skein of silk didn't lead him to the Minotaur: he held it in his hand as a last link with the outside world as he walked, farther and farther, deep into the bowels of the cave.

The Beginning of the Skein

As we drove through the town that Sunday evening I was excited. To begin with I was alone with Angela again, and we were doing something away from the unit, something the other film people would never know of, and perhaps never understand. Then we were at the beginning of an investigation of the accident. We were, I was determined, going to get to the truth about it, and this gave me a feeling of superiority over the director who, with all his talk about an eye for the exact reality of any situation, had quite missed, I felt sure, the significance of that dreadful morning on the cliffs.

It was odd, now I come to think of it, that I should not have remembered more clearly then the only time that I had seen the sergeant and his wife together. I kept it, I suppose, at the back of my mind; but I was feeling so strongly the harm done to the soldiers and Lil by the death of the sergeant that I thought of them as one common entity and forgot, at that time, their division among themselves. The soldiers had lost a leader, Lil had lost a husband who was, I imagined, supporting her. It was up to us to try and make what reparation we could in view of the true facts of the case.

I looked at Angela, and I had an unexpectedly long while to study her clear profile, her high forehead and the prolonged sweep-back of her hair before she felt the weight of my gaze and said:

'Sorry. I was just thinking . . .'

'What?'

'How I'd feel if I'd lost *my* husband.'

'And how would you?' I asked, and then, 'I am sorry. I had no right to say that.'

'You do worry, don't you? About what you have a right to say, I mean. I'd feel terrible, of course, lost, hopeless, dead myself almost. And yet when you were young did you never have a fantasy?'

'A what?'

'A fantasy. Did you never hope your mother or father would die and leave you alone?'

'Waiting for them to come home in the car,' I said, 'I'd worry if they'd had an accident; when I was a child, of course, it would have been the most ghastly thing in the world, and yet I couldn't help feeling . . .'

'That it would be a marvellous chance to do all the things you wanted.'

'I did feel that. Children must be very wicked.'

'I think so too. Of course, you never hoped it really.'

'Oh, no. I was always thankful when they finally arrived.'

'If only to have no more excuse for the horrible ambition. Yes: but say they hadn't come back?'

'It wouldn't have been like that at all, of course. Then you wouldn't have felt any ambition to be free.'

'Of course not. I'm only saying all this to try and understand how Mrs. Druker feels. It's no good being just ordinarily sympathetic. We must try and understand her.'

'Yes, we must.'

But at that interview she gave us very few clues.

We caught her just as she was going out of her front door. I can't say that she seemed particularly pleased to see us. She led us back into her front room and, without taking off her hat, waited for what we had to say. Since we were not invited to, neither Angela nor myself liked to take off our things, so we all three stood in the rather cold, cheerless room, like three travellers killing time in a station waiting-room. From the mantelpiece the sergeant himself gazed out of a wooden photograph frame; he was in the more formal uniform of the first war and had, in those days, certain brutal good looks. I reflected that he must have been considerably older than I had imagined. In that case he must have married late in life; his wife could not have been over twenty-two, younger, in fact, than Angela, and not, now I came to compare them, unlike her. They both had well-constructed faces; but whereas Angela looked entranced with her own beauty, the younger woman now seemed worried and tormented by hers. Her hair was frizzed into a number of nervous waves, and her make-up was applied without skill. Nevertheless she was attractive enough to make me remember her glowing appearance at the soldiers' dance.

While I had been looking at her, Angela had done her best to explain our mission.

'You see, if there was any question of neglect you'd be in a position to claim damages. We've been thinking it over and there are certain things that are difficult to account for about the accident. We realize that it would be painful for you to have to go in to them, but if you liked we could make some enquiries. We weren't at the top of the cliff ourselves, actually, but we could get some account of what happened from the people who were.'

'I don't want a court case.'

'It might not need that,' I suggested. 'If you had any sort of evidence, I should think our people would be glad enough to pay up and avoid litigation. After all, there's no harm in getting what compensation you can out of the Action Film Unit.'

'You use long words, don't you?' she said.

'I am sorry if I'm not making myself clear.'

'When I saw you at the dance I didn't think you'd be a boy for long words.'

Angela looked at us enquiringly.

'Since we made friends then,' I said, 'why don't you let us try and help you now? I know there's little enough we can do . . .'

My speech had its effect; she looked at me quite kindly.

'We feel so helpless,' said Angela, 'not knowing what really happened.'

The kindness died in her eyes. She turned on Angela and almost shouted.

'Why can't you leave us alone?'

'My dear Mrs. . . .'

'You're all the same, you film people, pushing your noses into what doesn't concern you, pretending to be very important when you don't count at all. He knew all about you. Who are you, anyway?'

'We're . . .' Angela started.

'You're not the police, are you? You aren't coroners, I suppose, or newspaper people?'

'Of course, we've no official standing . . .'

'Busybodies,' she muttered, and pursing her lips turned from us and altered the position of an ornament on the mantelpiece.

'If you feel like that, then, of course, there's nothing we can do. Only we assure you we came with the honest intention of . . .'

She turned back and stood before us again, her head hanging and her fingers twisting the fringe of the table-cloth.

'Perhaps you want a good story for your film? Well, it isn't a good story. He just fell off, that's all. Just fell off. That's what all the boys say happened and that's what did happen. It was just an accident, not a story like at the pictures.'

She sat down heavily and her voice died away. 'Put that in your film if you like . . .'

'We didn't come . . .' I started, and then realized it was useless to go on. She had sunk her cheek against the varnished wood of the chair-back and didn't seem to notice when Angela and I murmured our good-byes and left.

The whole interview had taken, perhaps, four minutes.

'I didn't know you'd met her before,' Angela said in the car.

'Yes. At a dance with the soldiers from the station. Rather a peculiar affair altogether.'

'Well, what happens next?'

'Nothing, I suppose.'

'Disappointed?'

'Of course not.'

'I thought you were longing to discover some horrible crime and disgrace the unit.'

'Not at all.'

'No more detective stories, then?'

'No more detective stories.'

Angela shook herself slightly. 'I'm glad,' she said.

Later. 'You're still worried, though, aren't you ? Over this business, I mean?'

'It's a ghastly business.'

'Of course it is. But apart from it being a ghastly business you're worried trying to fit it in.'

'It is a little difficult.'

'You worry a lot. Shocking as it was I shouldn't be surprised if it all turned out to have been quite straightforward really.'

'Perhaps you're right.'

'You think someone's to blame and you want to know which side you're on,' she said, with some astuteness. 'No one else bothers about it until they start getting blamed themselves, but you worry just because there might be something you can't justify. It worries me.'

'I'm sorry,' I said.

'Don't mention it.' She gave me a breathless smile as one wheel mounted the curb. 'I think it's very nice.'

When we parted in the lounge our brief careers as investigators were over. Had she been right and was I worrying too much? Had the shock of the accident in some way unbalanced me so that I was seeing phantoms round every corner, non-existent heartlessness in the Film Unit, non-existent hardships for the soldiers, non-existent perception in myself? I was tired and hurt, most hurt, I remember, by the accusation from Mrs. Druker that I was just trying to dig a film story out of her husband's grave; an intention of which I was, in advance, always ready to accuse the director. Well, he was on the look-out for the exact truth, and he had been presented with a most real event. Not understanding it myself I shouldn't be able to tell if he misunderstood it; and perhaps that was one of the motives for my investigation—the satisfaction of being able, at some time in the future, to prove him wrong. With the excuse that my efforts were directed to an ambition as paltry as that, I dismissed the affair from my mind.

Doris was having a farewell drink with Alec before he drove back to London, and they called me over to their table. I was glad of the distraction.

'You're in favour,' she said. 'The director's having a script conference to-morrow and he wants you to go along.'

'All right.'

'There'll only be the scriptwriter and Angela with you. The director thinks it'll be good experience for you,' she said, to impress me with my distinction. Again I felt this had been staged by the director in an effort to win me over to something, and again I felt a sort of hostility, a determination to preserve my independence.

'It should teach you a thing or two,' she went on. 'Although, of course, these script conferences never decide anything. The story's always shot differently, anyway.'

'Or if it isn't,' Alec put in happily, 'we can chop it about in the cutting-room so that its own writer can't recognize it. God knows what they pay writers for.'

'Especially that old phony,' said Doris. 'What the hell can he know about army life?'

'Something, I should have thought,' I remonstrated. 'He was at a military college.'

'About fifty years ago,' said Alec.

'And you know why he got chucked out?'

'He told me he had an urge to write . . .'

Doris laughed heartily and offered Alec a cheroot from a cardboard packet. When they had both lit up she said:

'That's just the line he shoots. I happen to know why he really left—heard it from a man who was an N.C.O. there at the time.'

'From whom?' I asked, puzzled.

'Well, from that sergeant, as a matter of fact. He'd got the scriptwriter's number all right. It was a pretty little story . . .'

Just at that moment a waiter passed and Alec started to negotiate for two bottles of rum. Doris's attention was distracted and I excused myself and went up to my bedroom.

There was no escaping it—at the end of everyone's story the grim figure of Sergeant Druker seemed to be standing like a sentinel. How would his part have worked out, I wondered, if he had never trusted himself to the rope on the cliffs? What sort of a figure would he eventually have built up to in the film? Villain, hero, brute or competent commander? Which side of his nature would have been used in the story, and which was the true side? With his future in the script to be decided to-morrow, it seemed difficult to think of him except as still alive, yet the one sure thing about the whole nebulous affair was that he was completely and thoroughly dead. And with this simple fact I thought of Angela's reassuring, 'I shouldn't be surprised if it all turned out to be quite straightforward, really'. But I was not reassured.

XII

The Script Conference

W E HAD OUR conference in the hotel ballroom, sitting round a table on ridiculous little gilt chairs which squeaked when anyone moved. The shadowy room, with its candelabra and high windows, stretched out round us, isolating our group, making us feel elaborate picnickers in a vast, empty field. The director was at the head of the table. In his silk scarf and leather coat padded with sheepskin and fringed with zip fasteners he looked like an exhausted explorer, most out of place on a wallflower's spindly chair. The scriptwriter also looked uncomfortable, he was trying to sprawl nonchalantly, which caused him to slip gradually away from us across the polished floor. He was busy filling his pipe, scattering a little mess of tobacco dust. Only Angela in her fur coat, sitting quietly with her note-book poised, seemed to fit in with the high mirrors and the parquet floor.

'In my bath at three o'clock this morning,' the director began, 'I had an idea.'

He looked round, almost nervously, at Angela, but she only took down in shorthand what he had said.

'I don't need a record of everything I say, darling. Only ideas for the treatment, or general notes for my book on making a documentary film. As I say, I had an idea. I was thinking about the accident. I suppose all of us have been finding it difficult to get it out of our minds, but thinking about it led me to ask . . .'

Now it's coming, I thought, what he says now will

show . . . I looked hard at the director, and he avoided my eye.

'Have we the right to disregard the accident? It is a very real occurrence, an important occurrence, and at the same time it is symbolic, it seems to me, of the war as a whole. When we get over on the other side we shall have to make use of whatever situation turns up. Now the point is, can we learn something from the tragedy we have been brought up against now—something that will give our story more reality? If we can, I say it's our duty to use it and not to hide it away.'

'I thoroughly agree,' said the scriptwriter, sitting up in his chair and sliding himself towards us again. 'I most thoroughly agree.'

'What do you think?' The director switched round encouragingly on me.

'I don't know,' I said. 'I don't know at all.' There was a wince of disappointment across his tired face.

'Symbolic of the whole war. Yes. You're quite right. It is symbolic,' the scriptwriter started, to cover my unhelpful reply. 'But just in what way, that's what we've got to decide. How do we want to point the symbolism?'

'Well, it's up to you. How would you handle it?'

'Let's see.' The scriptwriter lit his pipe. 'This sergeant has trained the men for the operation: everything they do over there will have been taught them by him.'

'That's what the captain said,' I put in; but no one took any notice.

'And the first lesson he gives them is in death.'

'Yes, but there's nothing heroic about the accident,' said the director. 'It's too quick.'

'So is all death in battle. No, the lesson must be drawn by the major at the funeral.'

'The major didn't speak at the funeral.'

'No. But that was because he was afraid of sounding theatrical. Not that his speech in the film would be theatrical. It would be very restrained.'

'Could you write us something on these lines?'

'Let me see.' Smoke enveloped him and his chair scraped back. 'The coffin with the Union Jack on it is lowered into the grave. Then we might use some words from the service, "dust to dust . . ." Cut to Ellvers looking up at the major, cut the major. He speaks . . .'

'Get this down, Angela, will you?'

"There's very little one can say on these sort of occasions. Any of us might have this facing us, and somewhere where there'd be no time to pay any tribute to our dying. Not that he wouldn't much rather have gone out with you, over there, without ceremony . . ."

'Perhaps you would work out the dialogue later. Let's get down to the story. Now, what about the accident?'

'He dies saving the life of the young recruit who up till then has been a complete failure as a soldier.'

They gazed at each other for a moment in silence. The director's eyelids came slowly together, and he sat for almost a minute in complete immobility. Angela started to translate her shorthand and the scriptwriter looked nervously over her shoulder. Then the director spoke.

'Good,' he said. 'It'll be very good. You've got the situation perfectly. Of course, it's only after his death that the men realize they have lost the most valuable life in the company.'

'And the recruit is filled, in a sort of way, with some of the sergeant's spirit—if that doesn't sound too phony,' the script-writer ended doubtfully.

'It isn't phony at all. It's human. In a way it's inspiring. If we tell it with restraint, just hint at it, you understand, it might be really effective.'

The director had got up and was beginning to pace round the table. The end of his shooting-stick slithered.

'And will you use,' I asked, fascinated, 'the real accident as you've shot it?'

'I don't think we could go as far as that.'

The director turned and spoke to us from across the floor. He stood in a shaft of sunlight, blurred and indistinct in the glare and dancing particles of dust. I know it was at me he aimed, in a final effort to instruct me and stop my futile and irrelevant objections.

'Art,' he started, 'even the film with its careful documentary approach, is not composed merely of slices of reality. It is the reconstruction of that reality with a selected emphasis which brings out its meaning.... What is so fascinating,'—here he sat down again and put his stick on the table. Angela sighed and seemed to be checking his speech with something already written in the front of her note-book—'in a job like this, is the thought that we are translating life in this way all the time, and even as it goes on around us. Of course, everyone does this to a certain extent, his memory retains certain "shots" from the past, junks others, he fits his glimpses into a sequence, chooses central characters. In this way the world outside becomes real and significant to him. Now, so it is with an event like this . . .

'The accident on the screen looks crude and meaningless. It looks less like a real accident than the accident that we will fake. Partly that's a physical fact—like the fact that Ellen Terry's robes were always made of painted muslin because real cloth of gold looked so stagy. But go further than that. A man drops down a cliff. What difference does it make to you that he drops down or is pulled up? The only difference is in what you feel about it. In one case you may be relieved for him, in the other sorry for his wife, and so on. We have to try to condition that feeling, and give it a place in the true sequence of your emotions . . .'

His face was very near mine and I felt it coming

nearer. I had to antagonize him somehow, to make him withdraw.

'But if your plan for the film is so rigid . . .'

'Yes,' he said, very tolerantly, determined to let me have my say.

'. . . that it tries to fit in an event where it can never belong . . .'

'Then one would be a bad artist,' and he smiled.

'I only feel that here . . .'

'Go on.'

'Well, to begin with, there are more people in it than you realize. It isn't just the soldier concerned with his soldiering, in this case. It's the soldier concerned with making films.'

'If you could just expand that . . .'

'Don't you see that if you hadn't told him to he'd never have got on to that confounded ledge? Moreover, it was someone's fault that he fell over and it isn't a question of emotional reactions any more. It's a question of someone being responsible for a bloody awful accident that ought never to have happened.'

I sat back and looked at my hands on the table. I found myself blushing; but I went on.

'Angela and I . . .'

The director looked from one to the other of us. It was an intolerable look which I can now only describe as quizzical.

'Your wife and I have been talking over the whole matter, and some things about it are still quite inexplicable. Why did the rope break just at that moment? And who was pulling the sergeant up?'

'And we found something rather odd . . .' Angela started; but the director had turned away from her. He spoke at me again, this time almost desperately.

'In a way I'm glad the question has come up in this extraordinarily acute form,' he started, 'because it illustrates my thesis rather well . . .'

I sat back, suddenly losing all interest in the discussion. Instead I watched the scriptwriter scribble something on a piece of paper and pass it to Angela. She smiled and nodded her head. The director went on talking.

'Of course, all the things you mention are important, they would be vital if we were defending an action for damages. Personally I don't feel we should be held responsible. Anyhow, our interests would be handled by our legal department competently enough. But we are sitting here to try and write a story, and from that point of view all this is as irrelevant as thousands of other facts about the accident, the state of the sergeant's teeth, for instance, or what he had had for breakfast. I know when you are young life seems so precious that you want to cram it all in; but as you grow older you find that the essence of Art is selection. Our camera's eye has travelled into many curious places and situations, and in most of them I have been careful to see that it remained shut.'

There was no chance of convincing him, particularly as I had no definite conclusions myself. Hopelessly I went on fighting a rearguard action for the facts.

'But you are opening your eye for this sergeant?'

'Yes.'

'Then how can you know whether you have got him in focus? What does he really look like? I assure you there are conflicting opinions on the subject. I have spoken to the soldiers and now he is dead they admit they have lost a good leader. But I have also learnt that a good many people had reason to hate him, and some to be afraid of him.'

As I said this I looked, quite unintentionally, at the scriptwriter and saw him redden. I felt sorry for what I had done but I went on.

'Even our people, who knew him, had different opinions

of him. From what I have seen I shouldn't have said he was
a kind husband, but his wife seems lost without him. What
was he really? Surely we've got to find out before we make
anything up about him?'

'With all respect,' the director was smiling all the time now,
'I submit that those are also irrelevancies. Everyone has as
many sides as a prism, every character sets going a thousand
stories. We've only got to tell one story and we can only
cope with one character for each man who has a part in it.
For your sergeant we take the character of an austere leader
of men who dies. You can't say that isn't the truth so far as
it goes.'

I couldn't. I said nothing.

'Is it worrying you that we are making light of this accident?' the scriptwriter asked me. 'Because we are doing the
very opposite, using it to pay the highest tribute to the dead man
and his profession.' He was quite sincere, and made me feel
more guilty for suspecting he would harbour a mean resentment against the sergeant.

'No,' I said. 'I suppose I was bringing up matters which had
nothing to do with a script conference.'

'Well, we agree on the shape of the story, then?' The director looked away from me at last.

'Yes. We shall need a new sergeant. Who are you going
to use—a professional?'

'I've an idea of getting Ellvers to play the part. He's young,
of course, but that might be a good idea. The young, enter-
prising type of non-commissioned officer of the modern army.
You know, that boy's a natural actor.'

'It's an idea. It would mean rebuilding the character, and
finding another recruit.'

'Will you go and see him?' the director asked me. 'See how
he reacts to the idea?'

'Yes. All right.' An excuse to get away from them all.

'Well, the weather's improving and we want to start shooting as soon as possible. You go and fix things up with the soldiers, and you get to work on the script. Angela will do any typing you want. I'll get Doris to work out a new schedule. You know, I believe we've really got something at last.'

The conference came to an end. We shuffled out over the slippery floor.

As I came through the hall I saw a remarkable scene between that bearded old hourly boy with the beret and one of Mrs. Henry Cooper's brothers who was standing, surrounded by portmanteaux and tin trunks, on the point of leaving the hotel.

'Good morning,' he said. 'My brother and I are just leaving. My sister remains.'

'Oh? Oh, good.'

'We go to unmarried cousins in Lyme Regis.'

'And lucky it was,' put in the hourly boy, 'that you met me before you went.'

'Lucky indeed, my man.'

'Gift of fate, I should say.'

'You may well say so.'

'If I hadn't been handy there's no doubt you'd have lost your whole wardrobe by the next station, never mind Lyme Regis.'

'I was able to let him have a length of rope,' the hourly boy explained aside to me, as to one excessively slow of perception. 'For his tin trunk. Fair bursting it was.'

'My collection of geological specimens, and the catch has never been safe.'

'Safe as the Rock of Gibraltar now.'

'I'm glad to hear it.'

'Good length of rope that.'

'Excellent.'

'You'd be able to use it again.'

'It will come in, I have no doubt, most conveniently on many occasions.'

'Five bob not too much for a length of rope like that?'

'I think it reasonable.'

The money changed hands. The other brother arrived with a taxi. The hall porter staggered out with the portmanteaux and geological specimens and the brothers departed. The hourly boy turned to me.

'Good morning's work.'

'Yes?'

'Helped the old boy out. Got rid of my rope, and made five bob.'

'Very good.'

'Queer how I came by that rope.'

'How did you?'

'Well, I don't rightly know. One moment I hadn't got it, and the next moment I had. Gift of fate, you might say. I take my box of tools out on the cliff one morning, morning of the distressing occurrence to be exact. I take out my box of tools and there's no rope in it. Lunch-time, I bring back my box of tools, tools all there *and* a very nice length of rope.'

'You mean, it just appeared there?'

'That's right.'

'Was there anything wrong with it?'

'No. Sound as a bell. Nothing wrong with it at all.'

I pondered this as I walked up the cliffs that morning, on my way to ask Ellvers what he thought of taking over the sergeant's part.

XIII

The End of the Skein

Having a good deal to think about and being, at the prospect of reopening so dangerous a subject, in no great hurry to reach the camp, I decided to walk. The way was easy enough; by now I knew that road by heart, almost knew the number of paces down the promenade, up the dusty track out of the town and between the bungalows, turning off on the path over the edge of the downs, past the Martello tower and along the cliff-top to the camp. I was walking the promenade's rubber pavement, reading the posters for concerts at the Winter Gardens, counting the wire litter-baskets and watching the seagulls swoop like trapeze artists under the broken arches of the pier, when I heard my name called sharply. I looked round and saw Daisy, the continuity girl, summoning me from the picture postcard stand in a kiosk.

'Hullo,' she said. 'Don't you think these are cute?'

She showed me three cards, all illustrating a repulsive flirtation between two babies.

'Very. I'm afraid I must be getting on.'

'Don't go, sonny boy. I want to talk to you.'

She paid for her postcards, cashed her sweet coupons, and led me out by the arm. I went with her curiously, wondering what on earth she could have to say, and remembering that once, at the beginning of our acquaintance, the scriptwriter had warned me against her.

She took me down a flight of steps on to a warm, dusty, heavily fortified patch of shingle, decorated with old bottles

117

and smelling strongly of dogs. There she hitched up her checked trousers, sat down and patted the stones beside her. I squatted obediently, resting my hand on a patch of dried seaweed. She opened her compact and shed a cloud of powder on the sour, saline air. Neither of us spoke, and I lay back, leaning my elbows on the pebbles. Daisy offered me a Craven A. I refused and threw a white stone over a tank-trap towards the sea.

'Going for a walk?' she asked circumspectly, and stretched out her legs, exposing, under the turn-ups of her trousers, silk stockings and little black high-heeled shoes. I didn't answer, but threw another stone.

'On a job?'

'In a way.'

'Going to see the army, aren't you?'

'Yes.'

'Doris send you, or Bert?

'No.'

'Have a sweet?' I accepted thoughtlessly and we muttered on.

'Nice to get a bit of sun.'

'Yes.'

'Hasn't been much like the seaside, has it, up till now?'

'I think it's been just like the seaside.'

'Cheerful, aren't you?'

'No.'

'Well, I can't blame you. It's been a rotten location for the unit, really.'

'I suppose it has.'

'Still, you seem to've got plenty to keep you busy. What are you going up for now?'

Her attempt to say this carelessly was too deliberate. She was worried about something, worried in the way that only Lil, out of all the people I had met since the accident, had really been. I looked at her sharp, determined little face, set against grey stones and the sea. I saw that she would get the information out of me as she had got everything in her life, the scholarship from the elementary school, the diploma for typing and the job in films. Well, there was no harm in her knowing; I was only curious about her motives. I answered as noncommittally as possible.

'Oh, the director asked me to take a message.'

'Oh, did he?'

'Yes.'

'Look, sonny boy. Who do you think you're kidding? The director wouldn't send you. He'd send Doris or Bert, perhaps, on a message of his own. The director doesn't even know who you are.'

She was trying gamely to sting me into giving a full account.

'Well, as a matter of fact he asked me to his script conference and after it he sent me on up here to explain a change in the story. I must really be getting along.' I struggled and sat upright.

'I suppose he invited you to the conference and not Doris?'

'That's right.'

'You can write home about that. Me, I've got some idea why you're going. You've got a little business of your own. Right?'

'What do you mean?'

'You know what I mean. It's you and Angela, isn't it, who are acting Sherlock Holmes in this unit? I heard you in the cinema.'

'You did?'

'I was behind one of the exit curtains. It's always best to keep up with what's going on.'

I was angry at her spying, and determined to snub her by explaining, quite candidly, what we had been talking about.

'Angela and I felt there was something still unexplained about the accident. We were anxious to find out what it was.'

'So that's why you're going up to the soldiers to-day.'

'Partly.' I saw no reason to lie.

'And have you, my dear Watson, got any clues?'

'One or two.'

'Very clever, aren't you?'

'Not particularly.'

'You've said it. I should think everyone in the unit realizes there was something wrong with that accident.'

Did they? Had this astute little creature seen everything that happened that morning, and were they all, perhaps, watching my fervent investigations with a sort of amusement? Was there a conspiracy among them to keep me in ignorance? Certainly I was angry at the idea, but if it was so, what could have been the point of it? And why, above all, was this girl beside me frightened?—for frightened, pale, trembling almost, she certainly was. I answered her as calmly as possible.

'I didn't think the director had much idea . . .'

'Everyone except him, perhaps,' Daisy admitted, 'and he doesn't realize half that goes on under his nose. Lucky for him he doesn't. His job is making pictures and he minds his own business; that's what we should all try to do.'

'But surely,' I protested, 'this is our business.'

'What are you trying to do, exactly? Get the unit blamed?'

'Not entirely.'

'Yes, you are.' She turned on me and in her anger bit her sweet in half. 'You've never been really loyal to the unit, neither has your girl-friend, Angela. She wanted to be a star, and you, I suppose, you want to be first assistant at the end of a month. You just want to make trouble, that's all. I believe you'd like to see the film cancelled.' In the way she said this there was not only venom, but a fanaticism even, which made it disturbing to hear.

' 'Listen.' I tried to persuade her. 'You say you realize there was something wrong with the accident?'

'Something, I suppose,' she admitted more quietly, turning her head away.

'Then don't you feel it's your duty to find out about it? Don't you feel there might be things more important than the success or failure of this particular film?'

'What do you mean?'

'The truth. The truth about the life and death of this man. The right and wrong of the thing. Surely that's important?' I felt that there were things I had to explain to her—things that, in the typing-class, there had been no time to learn.

She turned and held my arm, twisting her face and gazing up into my eyes. There was a self-conscious, childish appeal in her whole attitude, and I thought, with a shudder, of the flirtation of the babies.

'He wouldn't have done it,' she said.

I looked at her blankly. What was she talking about now?

'He's a funny type, you know. Can't get up in the mornings. Not much use for the unit. Sometimes he writes the most hammy dialogue. Maybe it isn't true either, the stuff he tells about his college. What if it isn't? Most people in films wouldn't like to have their past lives thrown up at them. They come to studios because producers never ask for references as to character. He wasn't any worse. It was just bad luck that sergeant being here, that's all. He wouldn't have done anything about it. Nothing like that, I mean.'

I was beginning to have a sort of dim comprehension of what she meant.

'I never for a moment,' I assured her, 'thought that he would.'

'You wouldn't want to get him into trouble.'

'Of course not.'

'Then leave it alone, sonny boy. Leave it alone.'

'I don't want to get anyone into trouble; but I can't leave it alone.'

'You look very determined.'

'I'm afraid I am.'

'Don't be afraid. I like it when you look like that.'

'Do you? I thought you didn't want me to go.'

'I don't. I want you to stay here. Stay here in the sun. With me.'

Without moving her eyes she twisted her body further round so that, still looking upwards, she was now lying back across my lap.

'You don't want him to get into trouble. You won't do anyone any good by going. Leave it alone and stay here. We'll pass the time, somehow.'

I couldn't speak.

'Don't worry. I am not doing it with anyone else. Not even with him. I don't think he's made that way, somehow. But you are, aren't you, sonny boy? You can relax, enjoy yourself. Why can't we have a good time on this location? Plenty of work, play in the evenings—that's how a good location should be. Why do you want to go getting us all into these messes? Leave them alone. Come on. Plenty of time, before lunch.'

'I must go. The director told me to go,' I managed to say. And I struggled to my feet.

'What's the matter?'

'Important message. . . . The director said . . .'

'Oh, go then, you little fool.'

I was half-way up the steps and I saw her turn away and burrow in her handbag. I knew she was crying, but I couldn't, with all the sympathy I suddenly felt for her and her fears, go back to her. I turned and ran. I ran as I hadn't since the cross-country run at school. I ran until the sweat poured down the inside of my shirt, my breath tore at my throat, my

stomach heaved and I was almost sick. I ran so that hair and
tears and sweat fell over my eyes and blinded me, uphill all
the way. I would have welcomed hedges to run through,
long brambles to tear my legs, ice-covered ditches into which
I might plunge and muddy banks to scramble up the other
side. I wanted a cold, driving rain and a wind that would
flap the wet running-shorts against my knees. I ran and I
wanted someone to cheer, someone to shout, someone to say
I had done well and present me with the unmistakable silver
cup. And at the end of the run I wanted a shower, no prep,
sausages, and a deep, guiltless, dreamless sleep.

But no encouraging housemaster watched me cross the
downs, no one knew what I was running to or why. I was
earning no conceivable honour by searing my chest and
punishing my legs. Stumbling at the end of it I fell against no
tape, but the wooden gates of the encampment; and looking
up I saw no congratulating judge, but the cynical, amused
face of the sentry, the officers' orderly, Wilkins.

'Rather exciting,' he started, 'like watching a messenger
arriving in a Greek play. I could almost see a cloud of dust on
the horizon before you appeared. Your unit should really use
the post or the telephone. A runner seems, after all, a primitive
method of communication.'

I could do nothing but lean on the gate-post and pant.

'I've always admired the enthusiasm you people put into
your job. I suppose film work is very fascinating; but no
physical endurance seems too much for you. Really, most men
in the army would expect a motor-bike or else walk. In the
heat of battle, I suppose, we might get that sort of sense of
urgency; but you seem to have it all the time.'

'I don't,' I gasped, 'usually run.'

'I'm sorry to have to tell you that your efforts may have

been wasted. I don't know who you can deliver your message to, except me. Everyone's out on an exercise at the moment. We're getting so much busier now, you know.'

'Are you?' I was grateful to him for talking while I recovered.

'Oh, yes. They've sent the only other corporal who really understood Culbertson to another station. Still, there's not much time for cards now.'

'Something big coming on?'

'That, as they say, would be talking.'

'I shouldn't have asked.'

'Quite all right.'

I straightened myself against the gate-post. This was to be my last conversation in uncertainty about the accident. Whether Daisy, with her simple boast of knowledge, or the rest of the unit with their rule of never being kidded, never taken in, knew the truth, I could not guess. But that this bland, half-smiling, gentle little soldier knew it—I was sure. The wind had dropped and there was a sudden, appalling stillness over the cliffs, the downs and the sea, so that Wilkins's answers, I thought, however quietly he gave them, would carry an infinite distance over the landscape and by their extension make inexcusable any further disregarding of the fact.

'And are you still'—I began, controlling my breathlessness, and so speaking more slowly, more carefully than usual —'are you still doing that rope-climbing on the cliffs?'

'You're thinking of the accident,' he answered, looking straight at me, and still smiling. 'No, we never really did much of it. I think it was something they put on for your benefit. In a real invasion, I should imagine we should all have been dead long before we reached the top.'

'Were you pulling the men up on that day?'

'With several others. It needed some strength.'

'I didn't see you, you know. I was down below. I often wondered how it happened . . .'

And then, as he seemed to hesitate, 'It's not just curiosity; if there was any neglect on our part it might be a question of compensation for the wife.'

'Oh, I didn't think you were being morbid. I was just trying to remember. . . . We pulled up the first one, Ellvers—he's a corporal now, by the way—that went all right. Then . . .'

'Wasn't there a tea break?'

'Yes. That's right.'

'Was the tea far from the edge of the cliff?'

'The urn was by the van, I think. That rather objectionable boy was serving it out. There was some dispute among your people about the price of sandwiches. I suppose we were there about ten minutes. Some of us were rather glad we had left the sergeant on the ledge without tea. He wasn't altogether popular, you know.'

It was so easy. I hadn't expected him to lie, but he was so anxious to help me; it was as if giving me the facts was a necessary act of politeness on his part, and no more serious than that, for he still smiled. But I pushed on, only just suspecting that his smiling helpfulness was dissolving, in some way, the solid ground from under my feet.

'And then you went back for the rope. Where was it, by the way?'

'Well, round Ellvers, of course. But he'd got it undone by the time we came back to him.'

'Ellvers didn't come over to the van for tea?'

'Let me see . . . No, I don't think so. No. I'm sure he stayed by the cliff resting.'

'No one brought him over a cup of tea?'

'They may have done. I can't remember it.'

'And the rope looked all right when you threw it down to the sergeant?'

'I don't know that we looked very carefully. I suppose we thought that if it had just brought up Ellvers it must have been all right.'

'And you noticed nothing strange about the accident?'

'How do you mean, exactly?'

'I mean the rope breaking; couldn't that've been avoided?'

'No,' said Wilkins slowly. 'No, I think that was bound to happen. The sergeant being, you see, the type of man he was.'

'Heavy, do you mean?'

'Oh, very heavy. Do you want to see Captain Verity?'

'My message is really for Ellvers.'

'Is it? Well, you won't have to wait long. They're coming back now.'

I turned round and watched the platoon marching towards us. I was certain now that I had their secret, only I couldn't yet be sure whether they were all in it together, or if Ellvers only had been guilty. He was bigger than the rest and he stood out clearly. If he was alone in his crime then the sight was terrible enough; but if the whole platoon, every one of these men who came at me in broken step with their sleeves rolled up, looking, their size slightly exaggerated against the higher level and the white line of the sky, like some fabulous and ancient football team, if they had all had a hand in this atrocious conspiracy . . . But the idea was fantastic. Ellvers had been alone for ten minutes on the top of the cliff; he could never have persuaded four different and decent men to connive in the crime he had committed. Ellvers alone was responsible, and I was alone in knowing it.

I must have time—time to sit down and think and decide what to do. I couldn't denounce him then and there as he stood with a thumb in his belt and rubbed the sweat off his face with a ball of khaki handkerchief. There must be people, authorities, I should have to tell, letters, even, that I should be able to write. Somehow, standing before the man himself

I felt ashamed, as if it was I who should have some reason to fear his knowledge of me. The captain had halted the men and stepped out to meet me. I was glad of the excuse to deliver my message, to gain time and cover the real purpose of my visit.

'We've had a new idea for our story . . .' I started.

As I had expected he looked only faintly amused and listened perfunctorily as I outlined the new scenes we wanted to shoot with Ellvers playing the sergeant who dies, and explained that we should need someone else to play the part of the recruit. When he heard Ellvers's name he repeated it and automatically 'fell him out', so that the man whose guilt I had come to believe proven was standing innocently beside us, listening intently to what I had to say and now and then glancing at the captain, as a child might look at its nurse whom it fears will tell it to refuse an exciting invitation.

'You fellows chop and change so much. Can't keep up with you. Well, Ellvers, we made you a corporal, now they want you to act a sergeant. Think you can do it?'

'I'll have a go at it, sir.' And he turned to me. 'Is it a star part, like?'

'It's a very important part.'

'Is it?' He stared thoughtfully at the ground between his boots.

The captain interrupted quickly. 'He's doing very well, you know; got a lot more self-confidence lately, haven't you, Ellvers?'

'I don't know, sir.'

'I should think he'd be your man.'

Ellvers had certainly changed, grown almost in stature as well as in assurance, and I began to wonder if the script-writer had not been right and he had not inherited some of his sergeant's spirit. But there was also a strange, new quality in him, so that he seemed almost deliberately posed, graceful and muscular as he was, against the line of the sea, and his gestures, even the movement of his features, seemed a little slowed down as if they were half the result of a conscious effort. Somehow this made me uncomfortable, and I was glad to turn away from him to Captain Verity.

'Have we Major Lambert's permission to start work on this new line?'

'Oh, I should think you could start. I can't promise you won't have to be stopped in a day or two. We don't know when we shall be ordered . . . elsewhere.'

'Yes. We understand that.'

'Acting another chap. There'll be more to that, I expect, than just being myself?'

'The director will tell you what to do,' I answered Ellvers coldly. I had no desire to discuss his part with him.

'And then, when it's all over—the film—will it go to all the cinemas?'

'Probably.'

'Give them all something to remember me by, eh?' I was shocked by a distinct note of pathos in his voice. The captain heard it too, for he frowned and said:

'All right. Fall in now.'

But Ellvers still stood by me. 'You'll be starting right away?'

'Certainly—soon as we can.'

'Certainly.' He repeated the word quietly, then shook himself and stepped back into the ranks.

The captain, too hungry, I think, to talk to me any longer, marched them off. As they left I heard the flatulent notes of the cook-house bugle sound from across the parade ground.

So I walked back down the same road, feeling the chalk, grass, sand, sea and bleached white houses press around me so intolerably that I was tempted to take a train that afternoon and put the whole complicated landscape out of my mind.

But it was as if I was carrying a grenade, due to go off in a certain time, and I had no idea in which direction to throw it that it might leave my friends unscathed and do most harm to my enemies. Nor had I a very clear notion as to who were my friends or enemies; I only felt I was alone, utterly alone, in my knowledge of the danger that I carried, and moreover that no one would ever help me to choose my direction, nor understand for whom I was fighting, nor help me to justify to myself or to the world those torn bodies which would have to fall on one side of the explosion which somewhere on this headland, stretching like a springboard out to the sea, was bound in a short unspecified time to occur.

XIV

Preparations

I<small>T WAS AT</small> such moments of intense and personal confusion that the placidity of the seaside hotel had, to me, almost an air of effrontery. As I came up to it that afternoon I heard the birds' chatter in the dining-room and saw the waiters move among the white tables like dirty merchantmen navigating an icefloe. Mrs. Cooper issued through the glass door into the sun, holding in one hand her long ebony walking-stick and in the other a small mauve parcel for the post. More suitably for my mood she had dramatic news.

'That director of yours,' she said, 'he must be an intensely patriotic man.'

'I suppose he is. Why do you think so?'

'He's addressing a meeting of your people inside. From the few words I overheard he seems to be proposing to lead some sort of personal expedition across the channel. Of course the news lately has been depressing and I can understand any able-bodied man wanting to do his bit. But will the authorities, do you think, really permit him to cross?'

'I don't know,' I said. 'If you will excuse me, I think I ought to be at his meeting.'

'Certainly. I must be on my way too. A parcel for my brothers. They're so careless, you know. One of their finest fossils, left in the bathroom . . .'

In the lounge I found the whole unit, including the hourly boys, gathered in one corner. They had pulled up all the chairs—some of them were even sitting on the glass-topped tables—and had denuded the rest of the room, from the other side of which the hall porter and the lift man were watching them with distrust. From the centre of the group I heard the director's voice, and as I got near and looked in between Bert and Doris I saw him standing up, leaning heavily on his stick and haranguing them.

'Ah,' he stopped and turned on me. 'You've got back.'

'Yes. Ellvers agrees to play the part . . .' They all looked round at me and I felt an uncomfortable distinction.

'Well, we've had later news,' the director interrupted me triumphantly. 'While you were away, the major 'phoned to say that he couldn't agree to our doing any more shooting as they expect to leave at any moment.'

So I should have to make up my mind; I couldn't let them go without having made up my mind—the thought nagged me incessantly as the director explained his plans.

'We shall have to shoot a lot more preliminary stuff somewhere in England. I'm going to leave a second unit behind here to do it. Bert, can I leave you in charge of that?'

Bert was the only one of us who had had any experience of fighting. The Air Force had broken his nerve with a horrible thoroughness, and consequently he was the only one who was really grateful for being left behind. Most of the others seemed to feel the job would be a sort of promotion for which they would willingly risk death.

'O.K.,' he said. 'Are you sure you ought to go over yourself? I may mess up the film without you.'

'I must take the risk. Sparks, I shall take you and a Sinclair camera.'

'Right,' said Sparks. 'La belle France. Here I come!'

He looked so frightened that I felt almost an affection for him.

'Now,' the director went on, 'I shan't need a big unit.'

'No,' said Doris firmly.

'We shan't need any hourly labour.'

The hourly boys were seen to shake hands and slap each others' backs.

'I was thinking almost,' he said, 'in terms of myself, Sparks and one assistant.'

Both Harold and Doris stared modestly at the floor and then venomously at each other.

'I'm afraid, Doris, that the major wouldn't consider a woman on the trip. I must have you handling Underling and helping Bert.'

Bert and Doris exchanged glances, ominous for their future co-operation.

'Before we go I want to shoot some stuff in the town with lights. The peaceful seaside town on the night the troops leave for the operation. Doris, perhaps you'd get that organized for to-night. Well, boys, I needn't keep you any longer. Angela, will you wait and I'll talk to you about packing.'

Bert stepped forward and spoke.

'Um, anyway, sir' (the director smiled) 'it's been jolly nice working with you. It's taught us a lot. I think we all feel that. And we'd like to wish you luck and a good trip and a good start to the picture . . . which we all know you'll make *the* picture of the war.'

There was a volley of clapping, and the hourly boys stamped a little.

'Thanks, Bert. You've all helped and if this picture's a success—I might say *when* it's a success—it'll be due to all of you, and not just the few of us who go across. Now, can I rely on you all to keep as quiet about this as you can? Right.' He nodded them graciously away. 'I'll just have a word with you, Sparks. And you,' he turned to me, 'if you're going to be my assistant.'

Once more they all looked at me with respect and I felt a shock and a sort of anger with the director for having singled me out again. Harold should have had the job—I had never asked for it. Couldn't the director see he was putting me in a false position with the unit? Especially since I knew what I knew, and had the terrible duty, before I could think of any-one leaving on the operation at all, of having to make up my mind.

'You're taking him?' Doris asked.

'Yes. I think he's come on a lot.'

Doris looked at me thoughtfully, decided just how much secret influence I might have, and came down on my side.

'Well, I agree with you. He's certainly changed recently—got more self-confidence.' Like Ellvers, I wondered, and felt in the midst of my embarrassment a sudden twinge of horror. Doris went on mercilessly: 'When he first came I thought he was another spoilt little intellectual.' The unit laughed mechanically. 'Good enough for a tea-boy, perhaps, for a month before he went back to his mother. But he's toughened up. I think he'll be useful to you.'

'I think he will,' said the director encouraging her, to my shame and agony.

'And he's good with the contacts too,' Doris went on more conversationally. 'We often get an assistant who can keep quiet, or organize transport, but we don't often get one that can handle contacts, particularly service contacts.'

'That's true,' said the scriptwriter.

'Do you remember Harry Hattersley?'

'Christ,' said Bert, 'do I remember him!'

'Little Harry used to put service contacts right off. I remember when we did *Naval Operations* he kept on telling the commander to order tea over the bridge telephone. Didn't do our contact with the service any good.'

'What a little rat!' murmured Bert, almost blissfully.

'But *you* know better than that.' Doris turned to me.

'Shouldn't be surprised if you didn't get a rise. Well, we'll leave you three to get organized. Good luck to you.'

They filed past Sparks, the director and me, smiling encouragingly but rather distantly, like friends saying good-bye in a hospital to a patient who is not expected, except by some miracle, to recover. Angela stayed with us and the scriptwriter also loitered apologetically beside the director.

'Excuse me . . .'

'Yes, old boy, what is it?' the director asked him.

'I suppose you'll have very little protection over there.'

'We shan't have anything to shoot with but a camera, if that's what you mean.'

'Exactly. I was thinking . . . I know you won't need a writer, but I have an old Colt, trophy of my father's, you know. Quite a useful little weapon. . . . In my day at Loamhurst I was recognized a passable shot. Sent to Bisley and so forth. . . . If you'd consider it . . . I should like to come along . . .'

'I'm very sorry old man, but I don't think the major would allow any more of us. Anyway, I want you over here to work on the story.'

'Oh. Oh, if that's the case, then there's no more to be said. Look after yourself.'

'I shall.'

'And you, young fellow. You've taken on a hell of a responsibility.'

'Thank you. I know.'

He walked stiffly away. By the doors Daisy was waiting for him; but he turned from her and went upstairs, steadying himself with a hand on the monumental balustrade. The director smiled as he watched him, and then he turned on us.

'We'd better only take a haversack. Put in sweaters, whisky flask, cigarettes, darling. Sparks, have you got plenty of stock?'

'Ee. I think so.'

'When are we really going?' I asked.

'Can't tell. May be to-morrow. From now on we must stand by night and day for a call. If a message hasn't come by six o'clock I'll shoot in the town this evening.'

'I'll go up and start your packing,' said Angela.

'Will you, darling? Fine. I'll have a look round for angles in the town.' And before he went he took my hand. 'Glad to have you with us,' he said.

'Well, chum,' Sparks announced, 'I'm going for a drink. Let me know when the ruddy little half-colonel rings up.'

I was alone.

Before to-morrow, perhaps, the bomb would have to be thrown. How could I sail with the men and such a danger among us? It would be like boring the bottom of the landing craft. I should have to do something; but how should I start? The police? I supposed my father would have said so. But I needed someone to advise me, someone who would thank me for asking them, who would convince me that I was acting rightly. (Even now, perhaps, I felt a sort of confusion born of the director's speeches, Daisy's persuasions and Wilkins's gentle smiles, and a doubt about what exactly, knowing the truth, was the right course to take.) I could keep it to myself no longer. Someone must know. The director? He was quite likely to dismiss the whole story as irrelevant imaginings. The scriptwriter? Somehow the recent hints about him, though so unsubstantiated, had lessened my respect for him. There was Angela. She had been in on the story from the start; she at least had a right to know how it was going to end. I would go and see Angela.

I went up the stairs as if I was a child taking a secret, too personal, disgraceful or private for its father's ears, into its mother's bedroom. The long, red-carpeted passage was dark. Angela's door was not open. In the shadowy recess of the doorway a man was standing, and as I raised my hand to knock he gripped my wrist and whispered: 'Come out of this.'

'What are you doing?'

'Come out of this. Come down here where we can talk.'

I followed him to the end of the passage, and we had, by a high dusty window flanked by the bathroom and w.c., an excited, confused and, to me, altogether bewildering conversation.

XV

Love

'YOU KNOW the director's gone out,' the scriptwriter began.

'He told me he was going.'

'So you came straight up here.'

'Yes.'

'You thought Angela would be glad to see you?'

'I thought she'd be interested in what I have to say.'

'You're very sure of yourself.'

'Am I?'

'Don't try and be clever. You're a puppy. Not been in the unit ten minutes and you give yourself airs, make suggestions about the script. What's worse, you force your attentions on a lady whom I happen to respect . . .'

'What do you want?' I asked him angrily.

'I only want to find out if you're still sufficiently uncontaminated by your friends like Doris, still decent enough for me to fight.'

'What do you mean?'

'As I thought. It's useless to talk of weapons. It only remains for me to kick you downstairs.'

'I don't understand.'

'You don't deny that you came up here to make love to her'—

'I certainly do. I came up to speak to her about an entirely private matter.'

—'or that she loves you?' he went on, not listening to me.

'I don't think it's very likely.'

He had been standing straight up against me, so stiffly that he trembled. Now he leant back into the recess of the window and gripped the dusty yellow muslin curtain, peering between it and the pane; his face was covered as if with a veil, like some old woman or curiously bedraggled bride. When he spoke again all his hostility had gone and he seemed to be trying to teach me a complicated theory.

'She loves someone. You can tell that. Obviously, she's made for loving.'

'I can only say that, as far as I know, it isn't me.'

'I thought it must be you. You're young. The director likes you. You're going abroad . . . Well, perhaps not. Perhaps it isn't you. But you must love her, a little. Come on now. Admit it.'

As far as I could see I should have given him no pleasure by lying to him.

'A good many people love her, I should say.'

'Yes. Yes. You're right there. A good many people.' He looked up gratefully, rolling up a great football of curtain. 'She's like an idea, isn't she? An idea for a play perhaps. You have a hint, a clue, of what it must be like; but you can never conceive it entirely. Not entirely. It's too, too complicated, and yet too simple at the same time. To get hold of it one would have to be more careful, subtler, more minute and yet bigger, stronger. I thought it was you . . . But I see now it couldn't be. No more than it could have been me. You know we're quite nice, you and I. Probably we're the nicest people in the unit. But we can't know her, can't really control her. We can be sympathetic to her, have kindly intentions towards her; just as we have good intentions in our work. Just as I had, once upon a time, a good idea for a play. We're not really good at our work. We'll never be. I never wrote a good play. Once—nearly, very nearly. But never quite, never complete control. That's the torture, to get a hint, but never com-

plete knowledge. When that happens there's only one thing
to do. Clear out. Give away your books. Get back to the
army. I couldn't, you see, after the mess I'd got into. That's
another long story. But about this business. I see I was wrong
to accuse you. Apologize . . . Perhaps there's no one—that's
what we shall find out in the end. That there's no one at all.
What did you say you wanted to see her about?' He threw
out a cloud of muslin before him like ectoplasm.

'About the sergeant's death.'

'It's all right—she knows.'

'What does she know?'

'All the sergeant knew—about me. But that doesn't make
any difference. Not with her. She's beyond that, quite beyond
it. She'd come to anyone, it wouldn't matter what they'd
been or done, if she could. I told her all about it. No one else
in the unit knew, of course.'

'I don't know what you're talking about. Angela and I
wanted to do something for the sergeant's wife. I came to see
her to discuss that.' I lied now, as gently as I could.

'She's very kind, isn't she? Where she can be. Naturally, she
can't be kind all the time. That would spoil her, don't you
see? In a way she has to be merciless, remote, like an idea.
It's my belief there's nobody at all. That's the answer. Do
you know, I made certain I would have to fight you?'

'Really, you had no reason.'

'No. That's right. I'm awfully glad. Always liked you, in
a way. Shake hands?'

'Certainly.'

'I'm glad we've had it out like this.'

And I'm glad, I thought, that I saw you all the time on the
ledge, for I should have hated to have had to suspect you.

'Nasty business, fighting. Stupid to fight for what neither
of us can get. Friends of mine once fought over a play in
France—such a damn' bad play too. You'd never believe it:

all about Helliogabulus. Decadent stuff. They wore dark shirts
so as not to show the blood. Melodramatic people. Well,
don't keep her waiting,' he ran on, still holding my hand.
'Only don't be so anxious to start picking quarrels in future.
You might get into serious trouble.'

He let go my hand, scratched quickly in his short moustache
and disappeared into the bathroom. With this mysterious
prelude I walked back to see Angela and lay before her my
conclusive evidence. I had no idea how she would take it.

Her room, when I went in, was very light. Certainly it
was one of the best rooms. The two high windows were
striped green and blue with the sea and the sky, and above
them looped curtains culminated triumphantly in the device
of the Princess Royal, who had given her name to the hotel.
Angela was lying on a white sofa, fiddling with her lighter.
In the yellow sunshine I noticed every detail of the room;
indeed, there was a suspension, as I looked round, of all her
movements, as if she were a character on the stage giving
the audience, just after the curtain had gone up, time to look
at the scenery. I saw her husband's rucksack, neatly strapped,
leant against the gilt claw of an armchair. Her magazines,
newspapers, letter-case, were littered over the bed in the
abandoned boredom of hotel existence. On the dressing-table
the sun polished the domes and minarets of scent bottles,
sprays and powder-boxes. Finally I saw Angela herself in
almost unbearable focus, a clear pattern of white and brown
with the dead cigarette in her lips and the thin chain of gold
slipping down on her forearm. Then I crossed the room and
looked out of the window.

'Isn't it a lovely day!'

'Angela, I wanted to talk to you. There are other people I
might have said this to, but I thought you ought to know first.'

'Naturally.'

Nervous of seeing her laugh at me I went on staring into

the bright, pantomime landscape of the sea-front. Peculiar: the wind, inaudible behind glass, seemed to shoot people by at a great speed. A boy passed on a tricycle, his feet hardly able to keep up with the speed of the pedals, and the script-writer, with the wings of his mackintosh outspread, also sailed before the wind. After him a newspaper raced along; it took off, flew over the promenade rails, and was trapped by the barbed wire on the beach.

'This business is going too far,' I started, firmly enough.

'Is it?' The voice came from behind me.

'It's time we did something about it.'

'Yes? Let's sit down and talk it over.'

I left the window reluctantly and sat on the edge of her sofa.

'I wanted to ask you before I did anything . . .'

'Very polite.'

'After all, I think you've got a right . . .'

'You're sweet.'

'. . . to know what I mean to do.'

'But,' she frowned, 'it's going to be so awfully complicated.'

'Nothing like so complicated,' I said, 'as if we just let things go on as they are without doing anything.'

'I see what you mean.'

'I mean that it must be obvious to both of us what's happened.'

'I can't be as sure as all that. I always find it much more difficult to tell. Sometimes I think I'm sure, but then I don't know whether I haven't made some awful mistake. You see, I thought the same about the scriptwriter, but now . . . now, I think you're right. I think we both realize . . .'

'I can't think why the others don't suspect.'

We were screwed round on the sofa, turned towards each other.

'Do you think they do?'

'They don't seem to. I think I knew from the first that it was Ellvers who had killed the sergeant.'

She leant away. The orange mechanical flame had sprung up in her hand; but she blew it out with a gasp.

'You think that?'

'I'm sure of it. Had you never thought it possible?'

'Yes. Possible. I suppose I had. Do you know, I thought you were going to say something quite different.'

'You thought I was going to say—someone else had done it?'

'No. Oh, no. I thought you had come for—something different altogether. . . .' She lit her cigarette and didn't go on, listened to me attentively and with a sort of obedience I hadn't expected; I had come for instructions and now it seemed that I was to have to give the lecture.

'It all fits in. I should have told you, of course, about a dance I went to with the soldiers. Ellvers was there with Lilian Druker, danced with her all the time. Then they were using her for a trick—a conjuring trick, you know, one of the men's a professional conjurer. The sergeant interrupted them and I suppose there was a quarrel.'

'So the accident . . .'

'It wasn't an accident. How could it have been, with the rope breaking just at that time, after Ellvers had been brought up perfectly safely?'

And suddenly I had no more to say. The problem receded with extraordinary, tidal swiftness, leaving us perched dry and lonely on a peaceful beach. It became a job, almost a routine job, that I should have to do some time soon. But for the moment this meeting with Angela, which was to have been an essential and decisive part of the whole business, became a break, a respite, a time off, and I was almost resentful, as if my holiday was being disturbed, at hearing her continue to discuss it.

'Why do you think he did it?'

'Oh, I don't know. Fear possibly—the sergeant was a frightening man; or hatred. I believe Ellvers had been given a pretty tough time. Or perhaps he was mixed up with the man's wife. Yes, seeing that she was so anxious for us to let the whole matter drop, I should say that was probably it.'

'In love with her, you mean?'

'I suppose so.'

'So what are you going to do?'

'I think I must see the major first—before the police, I mean. Would you agree?'

'I don't see that it matters.'

'I thought it would be a courtesy, to see the major.'

Angela sighed, and quite unexpectedly put her hand on my shoulder.

'It's not that I'm trying to stop you.'

To stop me—it had never occurred to me that she would try. If she did—the idea opened like a gulf between us and the suspicion that she was, for some obscure reason, not altogether on my side.

'We know what they did. What, I suppose, they're likely to do again if anyone else stands in their way.'

'What they did, yes, you found that out. But what are they like? I can't understand it. Can you?'

'No,' I confessed. 'No, I don't understand . . .'

'And yet, the other day, you were so angry with my husband and the rest of them because you thought they were misinterpreting the whole business. You were being very indignant and rather sweet, and altogether you got the best of it. They were making the men out as sort of heroes and, of course, they were stupidly wrong; but are you sure you realize the most important thing about Ellvers and the sergeant's wife?'

'What's that?'

'That they love each other?'

'Do you think that justifies . . .'

'No, not justifies. Must you have a justification for every-thing?'

'Yes,' I said. 'Yes, I must.'

'So you're going to see your major?'

'Yes.'

'This afternoon?'

'This afternoon.'

'And what will happen?'

'An inquest, court martial, I don't know.'

'And we'll all have to give evidence?'

'I imagine we will.'

'And so you'll drive the truth into all our heads—even my husband's?'

'Don't you think you deserve it?'

'I'm sure we do.'

She got up and started to tidy the room. She scooped up an armful of the books and papers on the bed and dropped them under the dressing-table. Then she stood in front of her mirror and did her lips, bared her teeth to rub away a little of the pinkness, and afterwards her mouth set in a sort of amused determination.

'Do you know, when you started talking I thought you were going to say something quite different?'

'What?'

'I thought you were going to make love to me.'

I got up, angry with her. 'Were you disappointed?'

'Not much. It's become a habit with people.'

'I never thought of it.'

'No. You were making great decisions. Planning exposure and cursing the unit's stupidity. That right?

'Yes.'

'You go on with your great decisions.' She put her hand on my arm again and looked up, smiling. I had a horrible memory of Daisy; but quickly dismissed it. This, I thought, is not the same. This will make no difference; afterwards I will still be able to do what I have to do, I shall be perfectly free, and as I was not sure that I wanted to be entirely free, the thought was a shadow. 'Great decisions suit you. You've certainly grown up since you came here.'

'That's what Doris said.'

There was a moment's stillness during which neither of us moved, and then we moved together. The sea rose up in the windows, the sky was a golden reflection across the white ceiling, the bedclothes billowed around us and I was resignedly, peacefully drowning, sinking like a stone to a cool, green, momentary death.

'Angela?'

'Yes, darling.'

'Are you in love with anyone?'

'Does it matter?'

'No, but that morning in the pub. Do you remember?'

'Yes.'

'You said you had to decide between—various people. Have you made up your mind now?'

'Yes.'

'Oh.'

'Darling, don't worry.'

'I'm not.'

'You worry too much.'

'Do you remember the first time I saw you?'

'Of course.'

'I gave you a chip.'

'It was very nice of you.'

'Wasn't it? I thought you were awfully greedy.'

'I was hungry.'

'I know. I suppose even now I'd be nothing to you against a great high tea.'

'What are you laughing at?'

'Something the scriptwriter said.'

'Oh, what did he say?'

'He said you were difficult to know.'

'Do you think he was right?'

'No,' I said, meaning 'yes'.

At last she twisted her watch round, ploughing the little diamond octagon through the gilt hairs on her wrist.

'Time for you to go.'

'You don't mind my going?'

'You must.'

'I'm glad you see it as I do.'

'Oh, I don't.'

'You won't let the unit know why I'm going?'

'Not if you don't want me to.'

'And I'll see you when I get back?'

'Yes. Oh, yes, of course.'

In the hall I met Dorcas.

'We're shooting all night,' he said, 'in the town. With lights.'

'I'm going up to the camp.'

'Oh, got a message to deliver?'

'In a way.'

'Overtime to-night. Worth keeping awake for.'

'Yes.'

'We've got to look out the hourly boys don't work twenty-six hours to-day.'

So I paid my last visit to the camp, my happiness beginning to be tinged with doubt, but my determination uncontaminated, resolute and built on the surest foundations.

XVI

The Major and the Minotaur

THREE HOURS later all the happiness and excitement had drained away and only determination was left. And then, as I waited longer, it became colder, more lonely, even sullen determination. If only I could have explained it all to the orderly, I assured myself, I should never have been kept hanging about like this; he would have told the major why I had come, and I should have been immediately admitted. However, I wanted the major to be the first to hear the news. I suggested sending in a note, but Wilkins said that he would never read it, he'd given up reading notes long ago.

Accordingly I sat on a bench in the passage and read the posters over and over again, 'Keep your Mouth Shut and your Bowels Open', 'The Enemy Watches', 'Careless Talk Costs Lives'. I lost count of time. At five o'clock Wilkins brought me a mug of hot, sweet tea. 'Run out of cigarettes?' he asked. When I said I had, he brought me a packet of Woodbines from the Naafi, and the *Daily Mirror* to read, as I might have a long time to wait. 'The major's just going to lecture us in the other Nissen,' he said. 'Probably see you when it's over.'

I read the strips in the *Daily Mirror*. After that I think I must have gone to sleep; because it was almost dark outside the windows when I got up and stretched and looked out towards the other hut from which the soldiers were just emerging, shouting and whistling and dragging their boots along the ground. The talk must be over.

They must be going soon then. That only made it more urgent that I should see the major in time. It seemed impossible that the soldiers could be going about their duties, making jokes, having supper, when I had a story which would bring them all gaping to my side, and only some unaccountable reticence of my own prevented me blurting it out to the first man I saw. So lonely and unnoticed, in that passage, had I begun to feel, that I think I should have started to recite my news to the air in the hope that someone would catch an odd sentence and spread it through the camp, if I hadn't just then heard footsteps and seen the captain coming through a far door. With some difficulty I attracted his attention.

'Hullo, hullo, hullo. Bit late for you to be out, isn't it?'

'I must see Major Lambert. I have a most important message.'

'Don't know whether he'll see you, old boy. Awfully busy, you know.'

'Wilkins said he'd be out now.'

'Oh, old Wilkins has got a bit out of touch. Still, if you like to wait until mess is over.'

'But I've waited nearly two hours.'

'Have you, really? Jolly tedious for you.'

And he left me.

This was all I needed to make me desperate. I turned at once and opened the first door behind me. I thought it unlikely that I should find anyone less helpful.

The first thing I noticed was a curious emptiness. It was the emptiness of a room that the owners have just left, after putting most of the furniture in store, to go on a long journey, perhaps never to return. And just as in such a room, after the removal men have come, even while the taxi is at the door, you may see a man in an overcoat collecting a few remaining trifles—so I saw the major now, stooping over the drawers of his desk, lit by a single naked electric light bulb. He didn't see me.

For a helpless moment I was tempted to retreat and close the door behind me. I didn't. I coughed.

He looked up. His face changed colour, lit and shadowed by the harsh glare from above him.

'I'm sorry to burst in on you like this.'

'Um,' he grunted, and if he had gone on talking straight away, standing up and twisted round in the attitude of a surprised burglar or a servant caught reading her mistress's letters, I think now that I might have not been entirely defeated at the interview. But he kept his head. He pulled up a chair and sat down behind his desk. He even gave himself an air of permanence by putting some of the things back into the drawers. Then he offered me a cigarette and we both smoked. He took time to set a paper at a perfect right-angle in front of him. When he spoke, he spoke slowly.

'What—what do your people want now?'

'It's not them I've come about this time, I'm afraid.'

'Well, who is it?'

'It's rather your people I wanted to talk about than mine.'

'What about them?'

He raised his eyebrows: he looked kindly, rather bored. I realized I must say what I had to with absolute directness.

'It's this. I think you ought to have an enquiry into that accident on the cliffs.'

'Oh, you do? Now perhaps you could give me your reasons. By the way, do have a chair, won't you?'

I sat on the only other chair. I had my answer ready.

'I'd rather not say what my suspicions are before you've thoroughly investigated the matter. It might not be fair.'

Again he raised his eyebrows without speaking, in a gesture, I remembered, which was also a favourite with the director. Then he said: 'You have scrupulous ideas of fairness?'

'I hope so.'

'And an enquiry, in this case, would satisfy them?'

'I suppose it's the only way.'

'The only way,' he leant forward and said deliberately, 'to

spin everything out for as long as possible, to cause as much worry, misery and inconvenience as possible, and to waste time, of which every moment is now absolutely vital.' His head dropped slowly out of the light as he spoke, and I was surprised at the eloquence he commanded, and by the fact that he seemed, for all his self-control, extremely angry.

'It's the only way I can think of to get at the truth.'

'I thought you people came down here to get a story. What do you want with the truth?'

'Oh, I realize you don't think much of us, and in some indirect way I suppose we may have been responsible for what happened on the cliffs . . .'

'Don't think much of you!' he exploded. 'My dear boy, listen to me. For three months my men have been training here—training under conditions of great strain for an operation so dangerous that only saints and athletes will be likely to bring it off. For this training their first necessity was peace of mind and quiet attention to work. At every turn you people spoilt this by alternately flattering and boring them with your wretched film-making. Now, by some providence, that nonsense is over, and you ask me to dig up an episode almost unbelievably painful and ill-omened, to enquire at nerve-racking length into the guilt and responsibility of each man for the death of one of their number, and this at a moment when any thought of death or failure in their minds would be worth a squadron of bombers to the enemy.'

'That may all be true about us.'

'It *is* true.'

'It doesn't affect my argument, but why did you allow us to go on filming after the accident?'

'Ah. That was the only time you could have been useful to me. After that the men needed a distraction, a relaxation of the tension. Ten days' leave would have done it, but by that time we couldn't afford ten days' leave. So I decided to let them think about film stories for a little while. Whatever silly nonsense you'd concocted about the accident it would be persuasive; you're clever enough for that, and it would have taken their minds off the real thing. Unfortunately, there was no time even for that . . .'

'I am sorry you've found us so unhelpful.'

'I tell you for the last months you and I have been waging a futile war which may end in the failure of the whole operation. It has been my business to make fighting look like a game, an elaborate and skilful football match with death no more to be regretted than a lost goal or a broken ankle. At the same time you people have been trying to light up the whole question with the flares of your lurid dramatics; if you'd had long enough at it you'd have turned my men into film stars, or, still worse, into heroes, so that when we got over to the other side I shouldn't have one decent, sensible fighting man who knew how to look after himself among them.'

'Suppose I admit all that, still . . .'

'And now that's all over, just in case the waste of time and the publicity and the distortion and self-consciousness of my men performing in your show should have left some of us unhysterical, you want to start all the play-acting of a court of enquiry with civilian solicitors snooping about, and perhaps eating in the mess and reminding the poor old M.O. about his divorce and getting us all worried . . .'

'This may be more serious than you think.'

'I can assure you nothing could be more serious, not even a general's inspection.'

And, like the director again, he gave a little shout of self-applause. I didn't laugh, but went on urging him, so that his smile died and he spoke to me like an irritable schoolmaster.

'If you'd only let me tell you . . .'

'I'm very sorry. I simply can't afford the time. I knew what it'd be as soon as they told me one of you film people was here.'

I don't know why this should have made me more determined than anything he had said before to persuade him. But I was angry, angry enough to go on, although the major was standing up to show me that, as far as he was concerned, the interview was at an end.

'It's not the film people that want this thing,' I said. 'They don't know that I've come here. They don't know any more about what really happened that day than you seem to . . . Oh,' I went on, overriding his interruption, 'you're right enough in what you say about them. I'd go even further, because I've heard them at script conferences discussing the whole business, getting everything so mixed that it would be funny if it wasn't so stupid and tragic. From the very beginning I knew that your job and your problems were quite different from what they thought them to be. Of course, I saw all through the sham story they made up about the sergeant's death. But now it seems to me that you've got a sham story of your own; you're no more anxious to know the truth than they were. You . . .'

'I know the truth,' said the major firmly, 'as far as it concerns me.'

'That's what *they* say,' I answered triumphantly. 'They say they're only concerned with part of the truth, and when you get down to it you find it isn't the truth at all. But please don't confuse me with them.' I felt I was arguing at random and I wanted to bring our talk back to the matter in hand. 'They don't know what I have found out. I've come in spite of them, and because I wanted to look deeper than their explanations.'

The major had taken the paper up from the desk and started to read it. Now he looked at me with more interest.

'So you've come here entirely on your own initiative?'

'Yes.'

'No one else shares your suspicions.'

'I don't think so.' Angela, I remembered, hadn't committed herself.

'And your director doesn't know why you've come?'

'I shouldn't think he even knows I'm here.'

'That's interesting . . .'

'I couldn't tell them. I could never have made them understand. They would have just thought I was trying to sabotage their position, out of jealousy or from some personal motive —they attribute the most extraordinary motives. Their film is the only important thing in the world to them—they can't understand anything else. That's why the accident was first of all an inconvenience to them—and then a bit of copy. That's why'—I was talking now only with the hope of holding him, keeping him back, preventing him from leaving me and forgetting me entirely—'that's why I don't expect I shall stay with them much longer. Surely a man's life—it must be more important than—than an idea for a story. You must see that, surely you must see . . .'

'So you came all by yourself?'

'Yes, as I said . . .'

'And you don't find your behaviour in the least suspicious?'

'Suspicious?' What, I asked myself weakly, what on earth was happening now?

'On the eve of a highly important and secret operation . . . because I can tell you now that it *is* the eve of an operation, you make an excuse of a cock and bull story . . .'

'An excuse?'

'Yes. An excuse for coming here. How do I know what for?'

'You can ring up the director's wife. She knows why I came.'

'No doubt a female accomplice. She had, if I remember, all the usual attributes of a beautiful spy.'

'This is ridiculous.'

'All spy stories,' he leant back comfortably into the shadows and pushed a bell on his desk, for the first time his voice did not sound unfriendly, 'are ridiculous. But they happen, every day.'

'Am I supposed to be a spy?'

'My dear young man, I don't know what you are supposed to be. All I can say is that your visit here seems extraordinary and I feel justified in using the authority of the Defence Regulations to have you detained under suspicion until such a time as you can do no harm.'

'But what can I know?'

'You've been here all the afternoon. There're all sorts of things you might have seen.'

There was a click behind me as a man came to attention.

I was in no mood to remind the major that all I had seen were the comic pages of the *Daily Mirror*. I went in silence.

Supper was served to me in a small office room off the guardroom. I recognized my escort. He was determined to entertain me.

'Was you ever a Buffalo?' he asked.

'No.'

'Pity. Lovely meals we used to get at Buffalo rallies. Pre-war, of course. First there'd be hors d'œuvre, and by that I mean hors d'œuvre, none of your little bits of coloured potato like I had at the Corner House last leave. Funny that last leave; the wife and I went to the Corner House and we looked at the menu. Why, you could read the whole thing through in half a minute. There used to be ten minutes' good reading in their menus, pre-war . . .'

At nine o'clock he disappeared. Then he came back for my cup and plate.

'We've got to be off now,' he said.

'Have you?'

'Another party.'

'Will it be a good one?'

'Jolly little gathering and another one where we shan't miss the late lamented.'

'You mean . . .'

'Here's Ruddy . . .'

Mr. Marvell bore a special message from the major. I was to be on parole until midnight, not to leave the office or use the telephone; after then I could leave as I liked.

'Sorry to see you here,' he said, 'but it's not much good opening your mouth to the major.'

'No.'

Jardine left to wash up.

'The boy's writing to Lil,' Marvell said. 'He told me to ask you how to spell "certainly". Wilk's asleep.'

I wrote it down and then looked at my watch.

'Two more hours to go.'

'Yes. Before *you* go.'

'Good-bye.'

'Good-bye, chum. I will now do the disappearing miracle.' Marvell leant against the door-post and then, bringing his left hand round the corner above his head snatched at his own hair and dragged himself out of sight with a ghostly laugh.

And that was the last I saw of the soldiers we had come down to film.

For a time I slept. Then I tried to reconstruct Ellvers's letter to Lil, to guess from one word what he was trying to say; but then I grew tired and thought, after all, it was no concern of mine. I walked round and looked at the scribblings on the walls, telephone numbers, misshapen faces, slogans cheerful and obscene, and in one corner the word 'certainly' written over and over again, spelled, every time, in a different way.

I became calm, contented, not even anxious to leave,

although the hands of my watch crept together. I had stopped thinking; the major, for all I knew, may have been right. Some spectre may have been deluding me all these days— and no one was to blame. I sat still and I can't tell at what moment it was that I knew for certain that I had been left alone. It was not long before I left the camp.

Outside there was a half-slice of moon, and under the cliffs a light mist below which the sea growled like a dog. The wind rose in the coarse grass along the path and wailed in the telephone wires. Among these sounds I probed until I felt a low, furtive murmur far inland. It grew louder, until it gripped the earth round me with a vibration that sang in my head, remorselessly as a dentist's drill. The cliff shook so that I expected chalk parings to crumble into the sea; but the land stood firm under the embrace of the great black shadows of the bombers which rose regularly from the clouds.

XVII

Operational

I GOT BACK to the hotel a little after one. The lift man was on night duty.

'Just taken your lot up. Dog tired they was.'

'They've come in, then?'

'Yes. Been out photographing the town, they said. They was wondering where you was.'

'Were they?'

'The female, she wasn't speaking any too kindly about you.'

'Oh?'

'Intrigue and malice; I suppose they're commonly found among them on the pictures.'

Under the slow scream of the lift's mechanism the sound of aeroplanes was still audible. By the time we reached my floor, however, the last flight had passed over.

'Something big on to-night, I should say.'

'Sounds like it.'

'Rather be on night duty here than there.'

'I expect so.'

I was surprised to see the light showing under my door; still more surprised to see, when I got inside, Mrs. Henry Cooper sitting up at my dressing-table, wrapped in a long red flannel dressing-gown with curlers in her hair, playing her patience between my hair-brushes. She must have seen me in the mirror, for she spoke without turning round.

'They've all been looking for you, my dear,' she said. 'They were working up to half an hour ago, poor things, and they were so sleepy. They heard from that nice girl that you'd gone up to the camp, and they said that you'd be sure to come back with a message for them from the major. So they wouldn't go to bed until they'd seen you, or rather they wouldn't let that poor child Dorcas go to bed. Really it was too sad to watch him yawning in the lounge, so I said I'd wait for you in here. I don't sleep very well nowadays, you know. I'm sure they're anxious to hear—have you seen the major?'

'Yes, I've seen him.'

'Good. They will be relieved. It's about some expedition, isn't it?'

'Yes.'

'Will you be going on it too?'

'I? I don't think so. I rather think I shall be going home.'

'Leaving this cinema business altogether?'

'That's what I have decided.'

'Why, my dear? Haven't you been happy in it?'

'It's not that. I don't think I am suited to the life.'

She brought out a small tortoiseshell case and gave me a rather dry, filter-tip cigarette. I felt excited and reluctant to go to bed. Past her words and my own I was straining for sounds from the other side of the Channel; but I could only hear the incessant sea.

'What will you do?'

'You know my father's always wanted me to go into his office. I shall probably do that.'

'Will that please your mother, do you think?'

'I don't know how she feels.'

'You know, my dear, your mother always thought of some creative life for you. Of course, she gave up her sculpture when she got married, but I think she wanted you to carry on something of the sort for her. Then, of course, her hap-

pening to have been to college with this director made her
able to get you in here. I know she was very glad she was
able to do that. After looking at him closely again this
evening I recognize him as one of your mother's old friends.
He has been nice to you, hasn't he?'

'Perfectly kind. But, in a way, it's because of him that I
want to leave.'

I said this without thinking. I was still listening for the echo
of explosions in the distance. They must have left at half-past
eleven. How long, I wondered, would it have taken them to
cross? As I listened the old lady told some anecdote about my
mother and the director, aimed, I supposed, at making me
stay with the unit.

'He was very fond of your mother, you know, and I think
she liked him very much, but he was always a little eccentric.
I'm sure it's quite a harmless eccentricity, and you shouldn't
let it turn you against him. Your mother never did, although
he did behave to her in a most peculiar way the first time she
met him. I remember the story perfectly now.'

'Oh, what did he do?'

'Well, she told me it was in the art gallery. She had come
to make a drawing of a cast by Praxiteles, I believe it was, and
she was on her way through the Flemish room when she saw
the director. He was copying a Cranach; I don't believe
students do much of that now, but in those days it was considered very good practice and the copy could usually be
sold in those shops which specialize in art reproductions. This
Cranach was, by all accounts, a most extraordinary picture,
which had always fascinated your mother, and she stopped to
glance at the copy. Then, as she stood there, the director
turned and stared, not at the picture on the wall, but at her.
He even seemed to be measuring her up with his brush. Your
mother found this alarming, and she moved away rather
hurriedly. Imagine her surprise when she heard, on the

polished floor, the footsteps of your director walking quickly
after her. It was a Monday morning and the gallery was fairly
empty. Your mother dropped her drawing-book and began
to run. The curious thing was . . .'

'What?' I asked, with a sudden premonition of what she
was going to say.

'He started to run after her—literally, you know. Apparently
he pursued her through the Italian Primitives, the Roman
Statuary and the French and Iberian Masters. Finally, she
managed to elude him in a little Minoan room which had
been started by the late Professor Sopwith. She was able to
crouch behind his model of a Cretan palace while your director
ran straight past into the department of Egyptology. His
behaviour was certainly strange, and yet your mother said
that when she met him again he was perfectly natural and
charming.'

In the silence which followed I heard a sound that might
have been a door banging in the depths of the hotel or a
thud echoing across the Channel.

'I only tell you this,' she went on, 'in case you should judge
him too hastily. By the way, I was to tell you that if you
had an important message, you were to wake him with it at
once.'

'Is that what they said? Then I'd better go up to his room.'

'Very well. Only I hope you'll consider very carefully
before you leave him. I'm sure it would have been your
mother's wish that you stayed.'

'I've thought it all over,' I said, 'and I'm sure I must go
back. I don't think I can have any of the characteristics of a
film director.'

'I think,' said my mother's old friend, as she packed her
patience cards away in their red leather box, 'I think that you
might have inherited some.'

·   ·   ·   ·   ·   ·

I knocked on the director's door and had no reply, although his electric light was also still showing behind it. I wanted to see him, and I wanted not to see Angela. Some words of hers came back to me. She, like the major, had thought I was wrong, and she because she was in love. Clearly her love had reached the point of decision, and for some reason I expected not to find her in her husband's room. I opened the door and first I saw an empty bed.

Then I looked round to the chair by the window. The director was in it; large, even larger than I remembered him, lit up by the electric light, lined about the face, asleep and fully dressed. And also dressed, also asleep, curled up like a child or a cat, with her feet on his knees and her head against his chest lay Angela, smiling. They must have come in too tired to go to bed. I looked at his face and I thought of the story of the two fantastic chases. Then a feeling, mingling pride and shame, crept over me, and I believe I blushed. I felt an instinct to go over and lie on the floor beside them. Instead I went to the window and drew back the curtain as quietly as I could. Low in the sky there was a glow, less natural than the cold light of the moon and stars, tinting the clouds in the east. They had arrived, and the real story was beginning. It was none of my business now. By me, at least, no story would ever be told against them. I was going home.

As I turned away I saw the director's eyes were open and his hard, blue pupils turned on me.

'Better get some sleep,' he said. 'We're all done in. Did you find out when they're starting?'

'They said . . . the major said . . .' Everything the major had said about the unit came back to me, but I couldn't have repeated it. 'You'll find out the latest news in the morning.'

'Good. Good work. . . . Clever of you to think of going up to make sure. . . .' He called me by my Christian name. Then his eyes closed and his hand stroked his wife's head, smoothing her long hair around her face. She had not awakened.

I lay awake all night listening to the sounds of fighting, and praying for the success of the operation which, although it was only going on some thirty miles away, might, as far as we were concerned, have been on the other side of the world.

XVIII

A Change of Plans

'A STATEMENT issued by the War Office says that advance units of our troops crossed the Channel just before midnight and were established on the beach-head early this morning. Casualties, so far, have been unexpectedly light.'

The birds hopped up and down in their cages, the sun shone and the waiter came round and administered a spoonful of marmalade to each of us as if it were a dose. Doris's smart little wireless stood on the tablecloth and spoke triumphantly.

'A strong bomber force gave cover to our landing-craft, and for a while effectively silenced enemy opposition. There can be no doubt that our forces had the advantage of complete surprise.

'And now we are broadcasting a dispatch from our correspondent who crossed with one of the specially trained spearhead units.'

Doris turned him off. We sat crunching our toast. Mrs. Cooper passed with her arms full of rations.

'Good morning. Wonderful news, is it not? I suppose some of them must have actually started from here—and none of us knew anything about it.' She smiled round brightly, but received no encouragement and withdrew.

The scriptwriter was calculating strategic positions on the back of the *Daily Sketch*.

'I wonder,' Doris started, 'if we've ever had such a mess-up made by an assistant director before.'

'Hattersley,' Bert remembered, 'never went as far as this.'

'Never had the chance.'

'You've had it, you know,' said Bert, and they all turned slowly to look at me, except the scriptwriter who drew a long black arrow across the map of France.

'I expect the director 'phoned Schwartz this morning. You should have your cards to-morrow,' Doris calculated.

'Only hope we don't get another arty little amateur.'

'Get someone with a bit of guts next time.'

'I don't really see,' I said, 'what I could have done.'

'You knew they were going. You could have 'phoned us. If you'd all been there he would have had to take you. The War Office had given you passes.'

'I tell you I was under arrest.'

'You could have bribed your guard to let you use the 'phone. You could have got the money back from petty cash.'

'I wasn't guarded. I was on parole.'

'Lad's bloody daft! That's all . . .' said Sparks.

'Christ!' said Bert.

Doris was altogether speechless. 'What did you go for, in hell's name?' she exploded at last. 'You were meant to be helping in the town.'

'I went to deliver a message of my own.'

'And did you?' Daisy looked up from *Woman's Own*, in which she had been nervously consulting her horoscope.

'No. The major wouldn't hear it.'

'Oh.'

'Couldn't even do your own business. What do you think this is—a nursery school?' Doris lit a cheroot. 'Well, the director made you second assistant yesterday. Guess you've got your job back, Harold.'

Harold smiled. The other assistant directors stared.

'Still,' said Harold modestly, 'I suppose the film will be canned now. Not much we can do now.'

'Certain to be, I should think.'

'Think of the waste of money.'

'And time.'

'And film stock.'

'All through one assistant.'

'He wouldn't be safe in any company.'

'It'd only be fair if he was black-balled in every studio.'

'I'll try and arrange that,' said Doris, 'through the trade union.'

'As a matter of fact,' I said, 'I'm considering leaving the film industry, anyway.'

'Hear that, Bert?'

'That's putting it mildly.'

'About time, too.'

'If only one knew,' the scriptwriter murmured, 'how much artillery they had got across, or even exactly where they had landed. Why not leave the boy alone?'

'Stick to your map. You don't understand the organization of films,' said Doris. And the faces of the four assistants turned vindictively on the scriptwriter, who clutched his walking-stick and was, I thought, about to strike Dorcas when we were interrupted by a page, who came zigzagging between the tables, shouting my name and holding a scribbled 'phone message.

'It's from the director; he wants to see me,' I said.

'I should think he does.'

'You'd better go and get the train home right away.'

'They say he's murdered assistants for less than this.'

'I want to see him. Where will he be?'

'That's your business to know.'

'In his room?'

'You ought to be able to find him at any time of the day or night.'

'He's probably in the gymnasium now, in Hope Street.'

The scriptwriter pencilled an address and threw it over the table to me.

'Thank you.'

'Mind his left,' said Sparks.

As I left the table Doris turned her wireless on again. I stood for a moment and listened.

'We have just received this communiqué from Allied Headquarters. Our forces have established themselves up to five miles inland. Opposition is strengthening and heavy fighting is expected later to-day. Meanwhile additional landings have been made at points north and south along the coastline. Our bombers, in spite of a certain amount of fighter and anti-aircraft opposition, are continuing to soften up enemy positions . . .'

The voice followed me into the street.

The town was empty and there was a noticeable absence of uniforms. The news was there again, chalked up by the papermen on their smeared blackboards. 'Strike in the West Now,' scrawled on a wall above them, seemed suddenly as tiresome and silly as the promptings which for the last week had nagged my conscience. I felt light-hearted, independent; as I walked I whistled. I thought of the director, regretful that I should have disappointed him. And then I realized why I was not apprehensive, why, angry as he was certain to be, I should be calm and unhurt and sympathetic. It was because we were so curiously near and because I had to leave him.

The gymnasium was down a side street near the hotel. Outside there were torn posters illustrating Sandow, and a door was open into a hall, a dark little passage, smelling highly of leather and plimsolls, and bitterly of sweat. The director's shooting-stick was propped against a radiator. I was glad that, in spite of what must have been a crisis for him, he was carrying on with his day's routine, and taking his accustomed exercise. I opened another door into the gymnasium itself.

It was a high, booming, airless, rather unhealthy room

lit by a single row of grimy windows and festooned with
ropes which stretched into the dusty air. Schoolboys in shorts
were suspended from a set of wall-bars, and they swung out
their thin white legs to the command of a master with a
whistle. In another corner two stout men were anxiously
shifting the responsibility for a medicine ball. The place re-
sounded to the clash of the director's single-stick bout in the
middle of the hall. He was playing a small thick-set instructor,
a last army veteran, I supposed, exempt from the call-up. In
their great basketwork helmets they looked like prisoners in
those newspaper photographs where the faces are always
smeared out; of the two, the director's body seemed younger
—even in the padded jacket it looked agile, nervous, and at
that moment possessed of a devilish power. He leapt for-
wards and backwards, swung his single-stick and struck as if
he was in the full fury of some ancient and desperate battle,
or as if all the failure and futility and hanging about of the last
month could be redeemed by a sudden, heroic energy. His
opponent parried his blows patiently and seemed to be waiting
for the attack to wear itself out. As I stood watching I calculated the director's age from the time when he must have
known my mother, and I realized how remarkable his performance was; at a particularly savage onslaught I hoped that
he wouldn't exhaust himself.

The schoolboys fell, like tired birds from telegraph wires,
on to the mat and were hustled out. The men left the medicine
ball and staggered past me rubbing their hands with handker-
chiefs. The director fought on, although his blows were
becoming more laboured. I heard his breath grating behind
the helmet, and the instructor began to press him back along
the strip of rubber. At last he dropped the point of his stick
to the floor and signed that the bout was at an end. When
he walked towards me he stepped quickly, without apparent
effort. Then he took off his mask.

I suppose we are used to seeing athletes—a cricketer walking towards the pavilion or a footballer running off the field —with their faces glowing and shiny with health. Certainly it shocked me to see the director still pale after such violent exercise so that his head, above the dirty white jacket, seemed as tired, leaden and roughly modelled as it did standing on the pedestal in our home. The infinitely cunning and leathery features of the instructor were revealed at his side. The director thanked the man, took a towel from him and gave him a loose pound note from the pocket of his flannels.

'Come into the changing-room,' he said to me, 'and we can talk.'

I followed him into a cubicle and sat on the lockers while he changed his shirt.

'I am awfully sorry this should have happened. I was trying to explain to Doris, there was really nothing I could do about . . .'

I stared at the photographs of boxers in long black tights, which covered the walls.

His head was covered with his shirt and he didn't answer.

'Perhaps if you got on to the War Office, there might be some way . . .'

I saw his face on its way up through the buttons.

'I've been on to the War Office.'

He went over to the cracked mirror and tied his tie, brushed his hair with the moulting brush provided and said quite cheerfully:

'I told them I'd changed my plans.'

'You told them . . . ?'

'Yes. We can't always be tied to their apron-strings. Now, in my bath at three o'clock this morning,' he swung round to present me with his new idea, 'I suddenly saw the film in quite a different light. I saw it as a studio picture.'

'A studio . . . ?'

'Yes. I was brought up to location work myself. Worked with Clayton, you know; we went to the South Pole, New-foundland, British Honduras. He always insisted on using the real people, and going to the real places. He was a genius, of course, old Clayton. I think you'd've liked him. He once spat at me when I suggested doing something in a studio: actually spat. . . . There's no one like him in films to-day. . . .'

'I suppose not.'

'Still, I think we've got a stage further than that all the same.'

He came and sat on the lockers beside me, took a rather loose cigarette from his pouch and lit it with a gold lighter. Angela, I remembered, rolled his cigarettes herself.

'There've been so many technical advances. As I told you before, we can make a thing look more real in the studio now than ever we could working on the spot. Actors, too, can behave far more naturally than the people themselves. And then, as to the principle of the thing, well, Clayton was very keen on principles; but I don't see that studio work is any more unreal, in principle; once you focus the camera at all you distort the subject, rearrange it, start practising the deception . . .'

'The deception . . .?'

'But you don't want any more theories. Let's get down to practical questions. I want to start reshooting in a month's time. Before that we've got to rewrite the script, engage actors. . . . I shall use the old story: the sergeant, the recruit, the accident—I think we might even try for a love interest— very subordinate, you know, and dying away as soon as the battle stuff begins. We shall need a girl, quite a small part: I might get Angela to play it—she hasn't done anything for a long time now. There'll be a hell of a lot to discuss and organ-ize. By the way—I want you to be my first assistant.'

'Me?'

'Yes. You've shown a lot of promise since you've been down here, and I want you to get an idea of studio working.'

'No, I couldn't . . . I couldn't do it.'

He had made the offer as if there could be no question of my refusing, and now he went patiently back to it to listen to any curious scruple I might have.

'You're thinking of the rest of the unit?'

'Well, partly. . . .'

'Don't worry. Bert's got to go anyway; with nerves in his state he's not capable of taking on the responsibility. If you don't like your assistants we can change them, and Underling's been watching for a chance to get rid of Doris for years.'

'No. No. I couldn't do it. I . . .'

'What?'

'I don't want to work on this film. I don't want to work in films at all.'

'But I can give you a start. Show you round the floor . . .'

'I know. But I don't want to work on this film.'

'Why on earth . . .?'

'I can't explain. . . .'

His voice, which in the excitement of his new plans had been vigorous and hard hitting as his single-stick bout, now sank wearily.

'Won't you try?'

I saw I should have to say something, yet how could I express my utter embarrassment and defeat? I knew I must leave him, just as I knew that, on the whole, I had better leave his wife because, in spite of our afternoon together, I should never be able to possess her completely, know her completely, or have her for my own. And he, he was my father, and not my father—just as she was my lover, but not that either; and this job was not my job, because although I had already swallowed the particular lie involved I couldn't bear to attend its slow, sickening, eternal elaboration.

I felt all that, and yet I couldn't say half of it. I knew I must only talk about the job.

'You said something about practising a deception. Well, we've all had a deception practised on us. I can't tell you the whole story: no one will ever know it for certain now. Perhaps it was necessary we should be deceived—necessary for the success of the action. But I can't believe it's necessary for anything else, even for this work of yours. I'm sorry, but I don't see things in the way you do; whether the way I see is more real or not, I don't know; but it's different. I don't belong with you . . .'

'You got on better with the soldiers, didn't you? Better than you did with the unit?'

'It seems I don't belong with them either. I think I ought to go home.'

'I can't persuade you? I don't understand you, I'm afraid . . .'

'No, you can't persuade me. I wish I could explain more clearly.'

I think I hurt him then. He gave up trying to understand me and ended coldly, 'I'm sorry. I was looking forward to our working together.'

'It would have been a wonderful chance for me, of course, if I'd wanted to be a film director . . .'

'But?'

'Really, I don't.'

'You don't want to be a director?'

'No.'

'No ambition?'

'I suppose not.'

'Very well, then.'

He laughed shortly and led me out into the street, collecting his shooting-stick on the way so that he could walk jauntily and swing and balance it like a sword as he walked. I felt there was no more for me to say, and he had returned to his most arrogant professional manner, calculated to discourage any further confidence.

All day the unit discussed rumours. Angela, Doris and the director disappeared upstairs. The rest of us waited about the lounge. Sparks brought out a pack of cards and made up a game of pontoon. Bored and rather depressed, I joined in and in a quarter of an hour had lost about half of my first month's wages. I was still regarded as a sort of lunatic for my inefficiency of the night before, but the unit was now beginning to treat the affair as a fabulous joke, to which my losing at cards only added a further ludicrous detail. As we played, various people would steal off upstairs and return with more or less extravagant stories about the director's plans.

First Dorcas announced that the unit had been asked to go to Burma and they should certainly sail before the end of the month. I never discovered the source of this story, and it was believed by no one except Fennimore, who immediately wrote home for a medical certificate which he said would prove him allergic to injections. Next the scriptwriter rather maliciously remembered having seen in a paper that they were to be taken over by the War Office entirely and sent to an army depot in Skegness. This led to Sparks abandoning his bank and beating about the lounge for the paper until Bert came down with the advance information that they were really only going back to the studio. Everyone seemed glad. Sparks returned to his bank, threatened to take me for a ride, laughed immoderately, and I lost the other half of my month's wages. Daisy read out that it was a bad business day for those born, as I had been, under Virgo, and everyone laughed still more. . . .

Finally Doris came down. She sat on the table with her hands in her trousers pockets and looked round her.

'Well,' she said, 'I suppose you all want to know the plan.'

'We're going back to the studio?'

'That's right. We're leaving this evening. No more free nights in this hotel for any of you. The film's not canned —we start to prepare for studio shooting to-morrow.'

'Same unit?'

'Yes. That is except . . .' By this time she was staring at me. 'You know the director wants you to be first assistant?'

They all turned on me. Bert lit a cigarette carefully, and the scriptwriter grinned.

'I've told him about that.'

'He said you had. He wanted me to find out if you were quite sure.'

'Quite sure.'

At last Bert spoke, quietly, gently, as if he was giving advice; but his eyes carried a desperate appeal.

'You say you're sure, old boy. But do you realize all the responsibility you're taking on? I admit you've done pretty well up to now—but being a fifth assistant or even a second's a little different from a first. A first has got all the worries of the film on his shoulders, especially in the studio. He can't afford to let up for a moment, day or night. He's got to be everywhere at once. He's got actors, extras, hourly boys to cope with, as well as keeping the director happy. Now, you've never worked in the studio before; why don't you try it out as a second for a month or two—the money's almost the same and you've got none of the headaches.'

'None of the headaches . . . !' Harold was beginning until I said, 'I'm afraid I can't do it. I have to leave the unit altogether.'

There was a sigh of amazement and relief. Then Doris asked, 'Got another job?'

'No. I'm going home.'

'Why?'

'Well . . .'

'But naturally you must go,' Bert put in hurriedly, and drew in his breath for another speech. 'It's obvious, isn't it? Why, we all hope you'll be very happy. I suppose when you first came here everything seemed a bit strange. Film people are difficult, you know, to get the hang of right away, and you were an odd sort of type to us. But now we've got to know you, and we're really sorry to see you go. Anyway, we wish you the best of luck. I suppose you are going back to get married?'

'Not,' I protested, 'at all.'

'Oh dear,' Bert frowned. 'Mother ill?'

'I don't think so.'

'Father?'

'I think my family's perfectly well.'

'Well, whatever it is I propose we should do the usual thing and whip round for a parting subscription.'

'Hear, hear,' said Harold.

'Let's give the boy a send-off.'

'No, really. I couldn't hear of it.'

'Bad luck about his father.'

'Poor kid.'

'Had to turn down a good chance on account of it.'

'Everyone give what they can afford. I suggest five per cent of your wages.'

'We had to give ten,' said Dorcas sadly to me, 'when Bert got married. And now he's having a divorce.'

Sparks took off his pork-pie hat and went round the unit as they opened the corners of their wage-packets and fished inside. I was too embarrassed to speak.

'Just get yourself something to commemorate your leaving the unit,' said Bert, handing me the hat with emphasis.

'Help to set you up in a new business, perhaps,' said Harold.

'Get something to make you remember us when you can't see us any more,' said Fennimore.

That, I assured them, I should always do.

They left me the bewildered possessor of two pounds, seventeen-and-sixpence.

'And this,' said the wireless, 'is the one o'clock news. Latest reports from Allied Headquarters indicate that we have made further progress on the north and south of our beach-head and that the whole operation is continuing according to plan. . . .'

XIX

Parting Present

I HAD DECIDED to spend my money on a parting present for Angela—at least on a present for her, for even then there was an obstinate, irrational voice inside me hinting that there might be no need for a parting, a voice which refused to take the sight of her in the director's lap as decisive. At any rate a present from me could do no harm, and I spent the afternoon wandering around seaside department stores looking for something which cost less than two pounds, seventeen-and-six.

I soon became bewildered among the berets, gloves, coloured powder-puffs and scarves, the smell of linen and the clatter of change shooting across the ceilings on little overhead railways. The record cases, musical instruments, calendars, plastic cigarette boxes were all too ugly or too expensive, and I must have walked miles between counters before I decided to give up for a cup of tea and a Hungarian band in the café. There, to my surprise, I found Daisy and the scriptwriter; she looked up at me triumphantly from her flan while he occupied himself, slightly embarrassed, with baked beans on toast.

However, he was the first to speak to me, and in his voice was congratulation and a sort of envy.

'Leaving to-night?'

'Yes, I think so.'

'You could almost stay on here for a holiday.'

'I doubt if I could afford it.'

'I suppose not. What job are you going into?'

'Life insurance.'

'Life insurance,' he repeated ecstatically. 'Ah, you're really getting out of it. How right you are.'

'I hope so. What will you do?'

'How I should like to answer you: coffee planting, sheep farming, tea . . . But I'm afraid I shall go back to the studio with them. I shall hang about the canteen. There'll be some reshaping of the script to do, and that'll give me a sense of usefulness until it's all shot differently. In the evenings I shall go back to Wimbledon and sketch the first act of a tragedy. It'll be good, but the second act will get out of control. There'll be Sunday work and no time for golf on Richmond Park . . . In about a week from now the director and I will quarrel . . . I shall write some bad-tempered dramatic criticism in a paper with whose Left-wing politics I don't agree . . .'

'Cheer up, dear, it may never happen,' said Daisy brightly, licking her spoon.

'But why,' I asked, thinking it kinder not to try to cheer him up, 'why can't *you* leave too?'

'It's horrible to confess it—but by now I'm rather interested in the film. Curse it, I know I shan't be able to influence it very much; I know whatever I write the director will turn out the usual slick, persuasive job; but all the same I'm attached to it—I want to try and do as much for it as possible. And then the next film will come along and I shall want to do as much as possible for that, even though I'm not at all sure whether the job wouldn't be better if the director did it all himself . . .'

'You know everyone thinks you're very good,' said Daisy.

'I'm not very good. There's only the feeling that I nearly was once, and I might be again. That's the devil that keeps you at it. It's the pursuit—like the pursuit of a woman when you humiliate yourself, abandon your home, career, get yourself in the most horrible mess; all things you'd never have done if you could have had her easily. It's very much the same, you know.'

'I suppose it is,' I said.

'Yes, my staying on is very much like a man spending months in an impossible house because the hostess is a beautiful woman.'

'Aren't you,' said Daisy, 'a boy!'

'And you're getting out of it,' he ended more cheerfully, 'for life insurance. Well, Jerry Vowles went into life insurance after his court martial, and a very good thing I believe he made out of it. Anyway, to celebrate your escape I shall pay for the tea.'

'No . . .'

'I insist . . .' And he made off to the cash-desk with the bill in his hand. Daisy and I drained our cups.

'Just tell me,' I asked her, 'what you meant when you said the whole unit knew about the accident.'

'I only wanted to scare you. They don't know.'

'And do *you* know?'

'Not for certain. Did you tell—about him?'

'I didn't get the chance to tell about anyone. But I know now—he didn't do it.'

The scriptwriter came back and we left the café. As we went out Daisy put her arm through his and sidled along gazing up into his eyes. I thought he was right to envy me.

I left them to carry on my search. In the end I bought a powder compact for two pounds ten, leaving myself enough for my fare home. I wasn't very pleased with my present, but it was at least plain and unornamented, even if it was only made of chromium. She will certainly have a gold one, I thought, as I walked back to the hotel clutching it in my pocket, and she will never use this. Presenting it to her seemed the grimmest of my trials ahead.

.   .   .   .   .

So grim did it loom that I decided to have a drink first, and feeling independent and forgetting that by now I couldn't afford it, I went into the back bar of the hotel, that amber-lit, mirror-lined bar where I had first met the director. And there, of course, was Angela, sitting in front of a double whisky and a bottle of ginger-ale.

'Hullo, darling. No dinner in the hotel, no food on the train. Everyone's madly packing. Nothing to do but get plastered. Have a drink?'

'Angela'—I put my hand in my pocket and then sat down and left it there—'Yes, I will.'

'Cheers,' I said when it came.

'You're awfully hearty to-night.'

'I'm leaving.'

'Are you glad?'

'Not altogether; mostly though.'

'Perhaps they'll feed you better at home.'

'Perhaps they will.'

We said no more until it was time for another drink.

'I'm afraid I can't buy one.'

'Why not?'

'No money.'

'Oh, I see. I thought they got up a great collection for you.'

'They did. I spent it all this afternoon. I had to buy . . . some things, clothes . . .' I ended desperately.

'Never mind, darling. I've got heaps of money. Two whiskies, please. Bung-ho!—or whatever your frightful expression is.'

'Are you looking forward to getting back to town?'

'I don't know. We'll have to have Underling to dinner, I suppose, with that extraordinary mother of his. And then I'm expecting a bit of trouble from the scriptwriter which is going to be generally upsetting. But I suppose we shall have

a few parties—three Canadian war-correspondents have asked
me to one at the Savoy for to-night.'
'What fun.'
'It should be. Probably get awfully plastered.'
'Probably.'
'Then I'm getting a part in this film. I shall enjoy that, even
though I know why he's giving it me.'
'Why?'
'The poor sweet's been a bit uncertain of me the last month
or two.'
'Is he—more certain now?'
'Oh, yes. Have another drink?'

'He doesn't want you to leave.'
'I know. Do you?'
'Well, I think you're a bit silly. It's an awfully good chance.'
'Yes.'
'Studio life's very nice. You've never worked in one?'
'Never.'
'Everyone's very friendly, good atmosphere, and then you'd
meet a lot of girls.'
'Girls?'
'Yes. You've no idea what power a first assistant has;
every little beauty queen who wants a small part has to
come and ask you for it. You might be a sort of Eastern
potentate . . .'
I was suddenly choked by a nauseating suspicion. Suppose
the director had told her to say this, told her to let the amorous
schoolboy know that he can't have you, but if he does what
I want he can pick the loveliest shop girls from Margate to
Land's End. He was quite capable of it. I stared at Angela,
but she looked entirely innocent.
'I bet there aren't many stars that haven't gone through the
first assistant in their time.'

The only way to stop it was to come out into the open. I gripped the powder compact in my pocket.

'I'm not interested in stars. Angela . . . I . . .'

'Yes?'

'If I did stay . . . would there be any chance of . . . ?'

'I'm sorry, darling. Let's face it. . . . No.'

'Then why . . . ?'

'Because I liked you, because you looked so hungry, because I thought you were going to blow the whole thing up, and in a way, although I should have hated it, that would have been rather wonderful of you : . . .'

'Are those the only reasons . . . ?'

'No. Because I thought I shouldn't have another chance—and I shan't.'

'Oh.'

'Darling, don't be miserable. You don't know what he's like. He's not the sort of man you can leave, or let down, or even deceive very much. He's got that sort of success feeling about him; no one can fight against that. He was born to be successful.'

'And me?'

'You'll be very sweet—in about fifteen years.'

Under the amber light I thought she had never looked so beautiful, so glorious and so utterly remote.

'Don't worry, darling. Anyway, I'd probably make you very unhappy. Perhaps it needs someone as selfish and ruthless as he is to control me. What are you smiling at?'

'Nothing.'

'If only I could have got away from him, I should have done it long before now—believe me. I should have gone home, or taken a flat by myself again, or left him for any of the people that I've . . . Oh well, give me a cigarette. You're not furious, are you?'

'No. Only tell me one thing.'

'What?'

'Did he ask you to try and make me stay?'

'As a matter of fact, he did. He's really very fond of you.'

'Do you think he knows that I . . . that we . . . ?'

'I don't see why he should. And yet it's extraordinary sometimes what he'll guess. Damn the man, there's not much you can put across him,' and she ended with a kind of pride.

'Angela!' It was the director calling from the lounge.

'There he is. I must go. When the man brings the change will you buy me some cigarettes?'

We got up together and she looked up at me, shaking back her hair.

'Yes.'

'Thank you.'

'Angela, darling Angela. Good-bye.'

'Good-bye. Look after yourself.'

I kissed her carefully painted lips.

'Get your regular meals.'

And she went.

I stood still and the waiter brought up her change which I automatically collected from his tray. Then I remembered her cigarettes and went over to the bar to get them. The bar was also backed with mirrors, and in these I had a full view of the room behind me, a deeper, warmer-coloured, cloudier view than ever. And at the door I saw, for the last time, the director.

He was looking at my back. Perhaps it was because I had just seen his wife in the same light that I thought he resembled her; but it was not only the light that suddenly softened and humanized him so that he seemed to stand there tenderly, nervously almost, gazing towards me. Perhaps he was not so old as I had thought, and as Angela had said, he understood a great deal. He might have come to ask me again, and if he had I feel now that I should have turned and run towards him, and gone bounding up to London in his long black car, and even given it all another try. But instead I looked down at the packet of cigarettes, and when I raised my eyes to the mirror again the glass door was shut and he was no longer standing there under the neon notice of the American bar.

In the lounge I stood behind a pillar, unable to cope with any more farewells. I gave the cigarettes to a page and I saw him run out of the swing-doors to where Angela was waiting at the driving seat of her car. In a moment he came back spinning a sixpence and I was jealous of his last sight of her. The rest of the unit was crowded out with their luggage, Doris supervising their departure, which was uneventful until one of the chambermaids ran downstairs to kiss Dorcas good-bye, burst into tears, and had to be consoled by the manageress. At last the hourly boys emerged from the lift behind me and as they went past they said good-bye, their rear being brought up by one of the riggers and the bearded carpenter.

'Cheerio, lad—good to get home.'

'More comfort in your own home, altogether.'

'Location's all right for the overtime; still, there's nothing like home.'

'East, west, home's best.'

'Not a mattress here like the old spring mattress at home,' the rigger was complaining.

'Can't find my sponge-bag anywhere.'

'They'll send it on, Slim.'

'Yes. Unless you've sold it like you sold my bit of rope I left in your box.'

'How was I to know that was yours?'

'Put it there for safety too. Fat lot of safety.'

'Now, Slim. Don't bear malice. Good-bye, lad. The boys are very grateful for the way you did our accounts.'

'Good-bye.'

They crossed the floor and Doris hustled the last one through the swing-doors. Hepplethwaite rolled up, took a pull at a small medicine bottle, drew on his driving-gloves and went out after her. Engines started like bursts of gunfire. Then there was silence. The unit had gone and I was alone. As a parting present they had left me one more useless and quite destructive piece of information.

When the carpenter had found the rope I had made quite certain of Ellvers's guilt. I felt sure he had substituted a faulty rope for the one that had just pulled him up and hidden the sound length quickly away in the carpenter's box. A rope calculated to break, yet not so obviously that the others would notice the weakness as they paid it out, would have had to be prepared in advance. Finding a good rope hidden on the scene of the crime had seemed conclusive. Yet if the carpenter's box rope had just been left there by a rigger and not by Ellvers at all, did the case against him collapse? Not really: but it was a further uncertainty. If I had been right there should have been a good rope hidden somewhere. . . . My speculations were interrupted.

'Sad. Very sad,' said Mrs. Henry Cooper beside me. 'It doesn't matter whether the run's been a success or a failure, it's always sad when it comes to an end. You've always made some new friends, and got to dislike a lot of new people. And then you've had another chance to find out how really very little you know about the stage.'

'Yes. You know I'm going home to-night?'

'You've decided?'

'Yes.'

'Well, give my love to your mother. Tell her I did what I could, but you weren't to be influenced.'

'All right,' I smiled.

'I shall miss having you people here. I couldn't make out what on earth it was you were up to half the time. I had the same feeling at those modern plays my nephew used to take me to on Sundays: people would keep on popping in and out, you wouldn't guess what for, but it was all quite interesting and fun.'

'I was just as bewildered as you.'

'Were you? I used to tell my nephew that the actors were probably like that too, only he wouldn't believe me. He said he thought there was some profound religious meaning in the whole thing, and they'd had it explained to them beforehand.'

'Well, I must go and pack now. I hope you'll come and visit us all at home.'

'Oh, dear me, no, I don't think I shall. I think I should make you all most uncomfortable.'

'Quiet now them picture people's gone,' said the liftman as he brought me down with my suitcase.

'Yes.'

'Proper circus they was.'

'Yes.'

'Director's wife said she was going to put me on the pictures. She didn't ask me to go with her, though. Still, I'm not sorry.'

'Why not?'

'Life of luxury—might have led me to form bad habits.'

'It might.'

'Not the same temptations in the lift business.'

'I should have thought . . .'

'Now then . . . don't let your imagination run away with you.' And he landed me on the ground floor with a grin.

I had left the hotel furtively, having had no money for tips. Certainly this was out of the way of the station, yet as I put my suitcase down on the thin grass of the cliff-top I knew I had only done what was inevitable in coming to the scene of he accident again. Not that it mattered now, not that anything further would happen one way or the other. It was just that I should have liked to have been right. I don't know why I should have felt so sure of finding definite proof.

The sun was setting, creating further shadowy hiding-places behind the gorse bushes and the patches of bramble. I searched quite aimlessly among the twisted roots and under the canopies of leaves and thorns, if I found it it would be quite by accident, there were a thousand reasons why it shouldn't have been there, besides the remote one that there had been nothing, after all, for anyone to hide. Ellvers would have hardly left clues about to satisfy my curiosity; he could have returned and taken the rope away at any time in the last week. Yet, for a little while, I had to go on looking. It was all that there was left to me to do.

I became less and less methodical, looking in the same obvious places over and over again. At one time my discoveries might have had some effect, but that time was over. Really, the part I had played had been most unimportant. I had not come to any conclusion; yet the story was finished, lived through, done with. In the studio and on the battlefront something quite different, advanced, removed, was going on, something which had left me behind, searching in the sunset, on the spot where the film people and the soldiers had played out their short, disastrous performance. I searched only a little while longer, and I found nothing. Then I stood up and looked at the sea.

It was a dark and leaden surface over which a crimson river had been spilt. The cliffs were a pinkish and crumbling white, and the flat grey clouds had pale bellies, reflecting scarlet, emerald green and blue. The lower sky was light and frothy and sunk into the sea like an oncoming breaker. It was time to get back to my train. I walked to the edge of the cliff and looked down, past my feet, past the chalk buttresses and deep pockmarks of caves, and saw the black edge of the tide risen right over the beach below me. I put my hand in my pocket and brought out my present for Angela. It dropped straight, and half-way down caught the sun's light. Even if it was only chromium it flashed like the most precious of metals before it hit the sea with a small, white splash.

The sky had faded by the time I got down to the station.